The Little French Bookshop

CECILE PIVOT

The Little French Bookshop

Translated from the French
by Deniz Gulan

HODDER &
STOUGHTON

First published in the French language as
Les Lettres d'Esther by Editions Calmann-Lévy in 2020

First published in Great Britain in 2021 by Hodder & Stoughton
An Hachette UK company

1

A CIP catalogue record for this title is available from the British Library

Paperback ISBN 9781529392241
eBook ISBN 9781529392258

Typeset in Plantin by Manipal Technologies Limited

Printed and bound in Great Britain by Clays Ltd, Elcograf S.p.A.

Hodder & Stoughton policy is to use papers that are natural, renewable
and recyclable products and made from wood grown in sustainable forests.
The logging and manufacturing processes are expected to conform to
the environmental regulations of the country of origin.

Hodder & Stoughton Ltd
Carmelite House
50 Victoria Embankment
London EC4Y 0DZ

www.hodder.co.uk

For my parents

Esther

Things didn't pan out quite the way I expected. I should have guessed after our meeting in Paris, the one time we all met up. They hadn't signed up for my letter writing workshop to improve their letter writing skills. Well, it wasn't their main motivation, put it that way. I soon discovered that this letter writing workshop was their lifeline, their only way out. It would rescue them from their trials and tribulations and help them grasp where they had gone wrong, mourn those they had lost, get their lives back on track, and rekindle lost love. Of course, I didn't realize all of this until much later on when I was already immersed in the intimate details of their lives. Why am I surprised? After all, wasn't it my lifeline too, after my father died?

I overestimated myself, assuming they would all be dying to write to me. In fact, John was the only one who did. I had envisaged myself being firm with them, but this didn't go to plan either. I couldn't do a thing with Samuel who wouldn't toe the line and refused to write to more than one person. I had also assumed they would be eager for my advice. Instead, they had other priorities and my words often fell on deaf ears.

I can't remember the exact moment I decided to put our letters together and compile a book. I think it was after the monologue exercise. Juliette hesitated before finally accepting, but Jean, John and Nicolas were immediately in favour, as long as I changed their names. Samuel agreed too but insisted that I use his.

I set about preparing for publication. This involved re-reading, editing, correcting and fine-tuning the letters, taking care to preserve each writer's individual style. They all have their little quirks. For instance, Samuel scoffs at repetitions, Juliette has trouble with linking words (as she does in linking the past to the present), Nicolas is blunt and outspoken (as in real life), Jean is hooked on interjections and John loves adverbs.

To make it easier for the reader, I indicated the names of the letter writers and their recipients at the top of each letter.

I wanted the book to end with Samuel, as he is the youngest of the group. I wanted him to have the last word. First, because I appreciate his intuitive intelligence and his sensitivity, which shine through in his writing. Second, because I see myself in him in a lot of ways. Neither of us were able to mourn the passing of our loved ones and bore a huge amount of guilt as a result. Finally, because I hadn't imagined that he would make so much progress in just a few months. Who could have foreseen that he would seize his life with both hands and display such spontaneity and generosity? And not just Samuel. John has also found the means to turn his life around. I like to think that my letter writing workshop came at a fortuitous time and changed their lives for the better.

Let me introduce myself. I am forty-two years old, and my name is Esther Urbain.

An Ad In The Classifieds

I was neither a writer nor a teacher, so I was going to need to prove my credibility to potential students. I planned to draw on my experience as a librarian of epistolary works and quote my favourites such as *Correspondence* by François Truffaut or *Letters to Lou* by Guillaume Apollinaire. I could also talk about the writing workshops I had organized in Lille from my own bookshop. These were hosted by local writers and held in the evening after closing time. With a subject like letter writing, I feared that my ad would merely attract lonely old people, who would jump at the chance to dig out their yellowed writing paper from their drawers and unravel their memories.

I had a clear idea how this workshop of mine would function. On 5th January 2019, the ad which I had posted a few days earlier on my bookshop's website appeared in four local dailies. When I had called the classified ads department of one paper, they had suggested I take the bundled offer to increase impact: *Learn how to get your thoughts down on paper, tell a story and talk about yourself by registering for my letter writing workshop. Participate from wherever you live. Runs from 4th February to 3rd May 2019.*

I got about twenty replies, from people of all ages, with a few more men than women. I gave each one the same pitch: *Esther Urbain, bookshop owner in Lille, librarian and copy editor specializing in letter writing.* I told them this was my first time running a letter writing workshop and that my role would be to help them write their own letters, while retaining their individual style and personality. I would rework their texts with them, and help them find the right words, to ensure balanced and accurate sentences. To do this, I would need to read their letters. I scheduled a meeting in Paris for the following month, just one, as I intended to provide feedback for each new letter by phone or email.

The oddest reply I received came from a psychiatrist in Paris called Adeline Montgermon. After asking me how the workshop would proceed and requesting references, she told me about a patient of hers.

"She's suffering from post-partum depression. Do you know what that is?"

"Err, no, not really, is it umm . . ." I replied vaguely.

She gabbled on. I gathered that her question had been a mere formality, as my answer didn't seem to interest her. All our conversations would go the same way.

"Well, let me explain. I'll keep it brief. If you're interested in the subject, I can recommend some books—you're a book-seller after all. It is also referred to as postnatal depression. It is a severe form of depression with multiple causes and affects the bond between mother and baby. My thirty-eight-year-old patient's depression was detected when her baby was five months old. She was initially admitted to a psychiatric hospital but was sent home before she was ready. Now she is being treated in a maternity clinic, with her daughter, several times a week. I do the consultations there, and that's where I met her. The little girl is now eight and a half months old, and her mother's condition is worrying."

I sensed a hint of annoyance in Adeline Montgermon's voice. I imagine she had opposed her patient's release from hospital.

"She claims that her husband wasn't supportive when she first came home. She has since reverted back to a state of extreme fragility, like just after her baby was born, and her anxiety and distress have resurfaced. I saw them both a few days ago. My patient quite categorically said that she wished to leave the family home and live on her own for an indefinite period of time . . . Without her husband and daughter. This came out of the blue; he wasn't expecting it."

"You mean they hadn't talked about it before coming to see you?"

"No. She wanted to tell him in front of me. My patient has difficulty finding her words and expressing her thoughts. She's very vulnerable. As for him, he has endured his wife's anxiety and panic attacks for months. He does what he can but feels powerless to help her. He is really struggling with what is happening to his wife. I suggested that he consult one of my colleagues, but he refused outright. It's a shame, but I'm not overly concerned. He's feisty. Time will tell whether the split is temporary or permanent. Though they have difficulty communicating, their relationship is sound. I suggested that they take advantage of this time apart to write to each other. Honestly, I have no idea what'll come of it. I think if they write to each other, they will be more receptive and actually listen to one another; something they are incapable of doing at the moment. And that's when I came across your ad. Perfect timing in fact. You see I'm afraid that my patient will clam up at the slightest hitch or annoyance, so it would reassure me to know she was writing to her husband via a workshop. Especially one run by a woman."

"What exactly do you want me to do?"

"Enrol them in your workshop."

"I don't know what to say, it's tricky . . . I mean I'm not a therapist and— "

"I know that. You'll treat them the same as you do the others. As for me, I'll continue to monitor my patient."

"But it'll mean intruding into their private life . . ."

"Like you'll do with your other students. That's not your problem. Rest assured, this will not be a problem for you, or them. Of course, I'm well aware that it may be tricky at times."

"Besides, I doubt they'll pay much attention to the writing advice I give them . . ."

She wouldn't take no for an answer, so I gave in.

I registered them a few days later once she had sent me their names. Juliette and Nicolas Esthover both sent me an email, a few hours apart. They said Dr Montgermon had recommended the workshop to them, but that was it. Four other people followed: John Beaumont, a businessman, who spent his life travelling; Alice Panquerolles, a hypnotherapist from Lyon; Samuel Djian, a young lad who had said by way of response: "Why not? After all I have to find *something* to do . . .", and Jean Dupuis, the most enthusiastic of them all, who you could tell from her voice was no spring chicken. I had hoped that there would be more participants. I noted with disappointment that not a single one of them expressed any interest in writing a book or had a manuscript lying idle in a desk somewhere. Shouldn't this be their number one reason for joining a writing workshop? Maybe letter writing arouses different expectations in people? If so, I would love to know what they are.

Finding a day, time and place to meet in Paris that suited everyone was no easy task. Only Jean Dupuis was totally available. She told me, laughing on the phone, that she was "as free as a bird". John Beaumont informed me that he would be out of town and could not be with us that day. We finally agreed to meet on 31st January at 6:30 pm, at the Hoxton, a rather chic, hip, hotel-restaurant in the Sentier neighbourhood, with an interior courtyard, winter garden and nice seated areas. My cousin, Raphael, had recommended the place to me. It was also an opportunity to spend two days with him, as he lived nearby.

Before our meeting, I sent an email to the six participants, asking them to think carefully about the following question: What battles are you fighting? If they were willing, the idea was that they would answer the question aloud in front of the others. I chose this particular subject because I'm convinced that everyone is fighting a battle of some sort in their lives and it is sufficiently open-ended that the person can approach it in any way they wish: they can be evasive and use a well-worn cliché, or take the opposite tack and give a much more personal, revealing response.

What Battles Are You Fighting?

nico-esthover@free.fr, juju-esthover@free.fr,
jean.dupuis5@laposte.net, john.beaumont2@orange.com,
samsam-cahen@free.fr

Subject: Getting started with our workshop

Hello everyone,

I was delighted to meet you all last Friday. It's not easy
to feel comfortable at these kinds of meetings when you are
just getting to know each other. That's why I would like to
thank you all for answering the question: "What battles are
you fighting?" You were all very candid. Below is a recap of
the ground rules, along with a photo of John Beaumont who,
as you know, couldn't be with us in Paris. John has likewise
received a photo of you all.

Throughout this workshop, you will each write to two
people. You can either write directly to one or two correspondents, or you can wait for someone to write to you.
Although, with the latter option, you do run the risk of being
left behind. If you receive a request and don't wish to respond to it, please let me know asap. I advise you to use your
first names. This will help break the ice.

During the workshop, you must only communicate with
each other by letter. If possible, write to each other regularly
to keep the momentum going. Try not to let too much time
elapse before replying.

May I remind you that your first two letters (since you have two correspondents) must include your answer to the question raised at our meeting: "What battles are you fighting?"

You can choose me to be one of your correspondents.

To be able to assist you with your letter writing, I will need to see a copy of each of your letters. I have noted that Juliette, John and Samuel will send me scans of their letters by email, while Nicolas and Jean will send me photocopies by post. Once I have read your letters, I will call you (Jean, Juliette, Nicolas, Samuel) or send you an email (John) to give you my feedback.

Later on, I will give you three exercises to do.

Remember that I am not here to judge your opinions, feelings or emotions, but to help you improve your writing skills.

If you have any questions, I will be happy to answer them. You have my contact details. Please note our workshop ends the week of 13th May 2019.

Ladies and gentlemen, on this Monday 4th February 2019, I declare our letter writing workshop open!

Speak to you soon,
Esther Urbain

Jean to Samuel

Verjus-sur-Saône, 6th February 2019

Hello Samuel,

I hope you won't be too disappointed to receive a letter from me. I decided to write to you as I miss the company of young people. I wouldn't blame you if you didn't reply though. At your age, writing to an elderly lady is hardly an exciting prospect.

When I was a piano teacher, I spent most of my waking hours with young people. Sadly, I no longer teach. If I had had grandchildren, my life would have been different. Don't worry, I'm not planning to make you my surrogate grandchild. This is the course my life has taken and I'm resigned to it. Funnily enough, people who make fatalistic statements like "embrace your fate" or "it's your destiny" infuriate me. Yet here I am doing the same, though I don't mean a word of it. I don't have grandchildren, but wish I did, it's unfair. There you go! I don't suppose you'll believe me if I tell you that I'm not a lonely old lady, but it's true. I've got friends, lots of animals, and I'm very active . . . And, you know what? Living alone isn't all that bad.

What did you think of our meeting? I thought we all appeared ill at ease. We hardly dared look each other in the face, or even smile. It reminded me of the first day of school, when you sneak a peek at the other pupils feeling curious and wary all at once. To my surprise, when Esther asked us to answer that question we all bared our souls. I remember you said you were "fighting against the urge to smash everything up". Ouch! You've got your whole life ahead of you, young man. You seem like an intelligent lad, you've got all your mental and physical faculties, and on top of that you're a looker! So why such a cynical

response? You arrived late, dragging your feet as if you
had been forced to come. Eyes glued to your phone. I'm
surprised you even noticed us! I'm not judging you. I simply concluded that you didn't come of your own accord.
As for me, you probably don't remember, but I replied
that I was fighting a battle against anger. My reply was so
frank, I was worried it wouldn't go down well. As it turned
out, everyone's replies were as sinister as mine (quite funny, when you think about it!), so I blended right in with
the general doom and gloom.

I hope you write back. I would be delighted to hear from
you.

Best wishes,
Jean

Jean puts down her pencil. She'll re-read it later. Was she
too direct? Should she tone it down? She's convinced that
Samuel will quit the workshop at the slightest excuse or if
he has to make any sort of effort. He may even have quit
after the meeting, deciding that it wasn't for him. At the
Hoxton, she had seen him arriving from a distance. At first,
she hadn't realized that this was the young man they were
waiting for. They were already seated at the back of the
first reception room, near the bar. After he passed through
the double-door entrance, he stopped dead in his tracks.
The hood of his fleece was pulled up over his head, and he
was clad in jeans and white trainers. You could read him
like an open book. He wasn't used to that kind of place.
Intimidated by the decor, he was already on the defensive
and didn't dare look around him. The eighteenth-century
private mansion, a listed building with its winter garden,
botanical wall and interior courtyards, was certainly impressive. It was the kind of place where business people

meet to discuss digital culture, media, public relations and sustainable development. Parisians and fashionable tourists go there to sip cocktails and show off their designer bumbags, the latest must-have accessory, by Prada, Dior, Vuitton or Gucci. People sit in small cosy groups; it's all very *casual chic*.

If it weren't for her friend Luc, the owner of the bistro in the village where she drinks her coffee every morning, she would never have known about Esther's ad in the local paper. Luc had thought that the idea of a letter writing workshop was "*strange*". He could "*smell a rat*". But that morning, she didn't pull him up on his annoying habit of throwing in anglicisms any chance he got. Knowing how touchy and sensitive he was, she had learnt to hold her tongue. As she had copied out the small ad into her notebook, Luc had urged caution, despite knowing she wouldn't listen and was as stubborn as a mule. Developers and estate agents had been coveting her house for a while now. They had offered her twice the going rate for the area. "You shouldn't let this opportunity pass you by, Mrs Dupuis," they remarked each time. They had even offered to help her find a new home nearby if she wished, somewhere more modern and comfortable. One day, one of them had praised the virtues of having a "nice cosy little home". Jean had been furious, retorting that she hated anything "cosy". To her, *cosy* was synonymous with softness, cocooning, and suffocation. Anathema to someone who loves natural things and vast, wide open spaces. She had asked if he understood where she was coming from, and he had admitted that he didn't. "Stop thinking that senior citizens want everything to be *cosy*," she had bellowed. He had left without insisting. She had stood her ground ever since, refusing to move and preventing further work on the Great Meadows development. After her

initial astonishment, Jean, tickled pink at this grandiose
name, had roared with laughter. She hadn't hesitated to
ask the right-wing mayor of her village where these "great
meadows" were. Pierre Darguemarche had replied that he
had nothing to do with the names given to the housing
estates. Jean deemed their design "lazy" from an archi-
tectural and aesthetic point of view. In just a few weeks,
she had witnessed the emergence of eight white plastered
cubes, lined up next to each other on the side of the road,
like soldiers, then a second row just like the first. Tearing
her house down would have allowed a third row of uni-
form white monstrosities to be built. They were separated by a white gravel driveway containing tall grey plastic planters every five metres in which laurel trees were
planted, only to die from casual neglect. The ficus trees
that succeeded them met with the same sad fate. Now,
the planters served as meeting points and ashtrays for local youths. "The highlight of the show", as Jean put it,
was the PVC gates, adorned with scrolls and ostentatious
looking medallions, which one would expect to find at the
entrance to a manor house rather than a housing estate.
Not a trace was left of Martine and Jacques Bazoche's
poor vineyards, which had been sold off to the highest
bidder who had convinced them they were lucky to have
been made such a wonderful offer. After the sale, the Ba-
zoches moved to the southeast of France. Every time there
was torrential rain on the French Riviera, Jean couldn't
stop herself from gloating. And this was just the start,
she rejoiced privately, imagining the ex-winegrowers up
to their necks in floodwater. She loved telling people that
they scarpered before the bulldozers began demolishing
their beautiful house and vineyards. They hadn't wanted
to watch the shovels rip their vines out of the ground. Jean
had cried, even though it wasn't her land. She wouldn't

sell hers. The prospect of her old stone house being razed to the ground was unbearable. At least some of the inhabitants of Great Meadows still had a view of her garden and vineyards. But Jean blames the mayor, not them. They are simply delighted at being first-time homeowners, you can see it in their faces. They even seem to find the uniformity of the garages, gardens, façades and shutters reassuring. The mayor, with two terms under his belt, doesn't know what the fuss is about. As long as the local population is growing and the primary schools are not threatened with closure, what does it matter? Any small shops left in Verjus owe their lucky fate to him. Jean understands his stance, but why build such ugly looking buildings? She is still mad about the 1977 property law which stipulates that you don't have to use an architect for the construction or renovation of buildings with a surface area of less than one hundred and seventy square metres. But there's nothing she can do about it.

Industrial estates and retail parks are her second pet hate. On this subject she doesn't mince her words. She tells anyone who'll listen that no one seems to give a damn that these drab, soulless eyesores are destroying small businesses in villages and towns, that they are ugly and depressing even if they are considered to be practical because you can find all the shops you need at the same location. Plus you need a car to get to these restaurants, hypermarkets, garden centres, furniture, sports and DIY stores. Jean is disgusted that for the sake of saving a bit of time, shoppers are willing to sacrifice traditions and other peoples' livelihoods, following fashions like a herd of sheep. Jean is alarmed by this division of life into commercial, residential, industrial and leisure zones.

She photocopies her letter and heads to the post office. She sends it to Samuel's address in Villejuif, with a copy to Esther in Lille.

*

As for Samuel, he'd promised Ben that he would drop by the restaurant in the morning to return his backpack. By the time he picked up his post he had already forgotten about the workshop meeting a week earlier. Jean's letter refreshed his memory. He read it while walking down the street. He realized he'd have to reply as he hadn't written to anyone in the group. If he quits now, his mother will be furious, as she is already running out of patience. He would have preferred to hear from that businessman, John Beaumont. He had even hoped that he would take him under his wing and give him a job, though Samuel had made no actual effort to make this happen.

"Serves me sodding well right," he grumbles as he pushes open the door of the restaurant. "I don't even know what the bloke does for a living!" It's not too late to write to him, but Samuel knows he won't bother. For the past year and a half, he has been exceedingly laid back, taking things as they come. He has no control over his life, no plans, expects nothing, and hopes for nothing. He doesn't feel entitled to ask anything of anyone, not wishing to take the place of someone more deserving.

Ben is peeling potatoes. "I'm not planning on rotting in this dump for long, bro," he says to Samuel, looking moody. "Wanna coffee?"

"Yeah . . . please. Here's your bag."

"Cheers. What yer doing here anyway?"

"Nothing much. Goin' to the supermarket for my mum. Can you give me a napkin?"

"Err . . . yeah, what for?"

"I gotta write a letter."

"A letter? Can't you just send an email?"

"Nope . . . Long story."

"Here . . . Right, I got to get back to the potatoes before that other idiot gets back."

"You comin' round tomorrow night for *Game of Thrones*?"
"Yeah . . . Laters."

Samuel to Jean

15th February

Hello Jean,
   I'm happy to write to you, even if I have no idea what we're going to talk about. Sorry about the napkin, I didn't have any writing paper. I'm going to buy a notepad but I realized that if I didn't reply to you right away, I probably wouldn't do it later. You're right, I didn't want to come. My mum made it clear that if I didn't find something to do she was going to make me work at the local supermarket. She heard they were looking for people. I can think of nothing worse. I saw the ad in the local paper that my dad gets and I told my mum I quite liked the idea of joining the workshop. She was really pleased as she thinks I'm good at writing (by that she means I'm a good speller) and that it might help me to write down everything that's wrong in my life. She says it'll make me feel better.
   Last year, she sent me to see a therapist, but it didn't work out. He was a nice guy, that wasn't the problem. What annoyed me was that nothing I told him surprised him. He knew everything already. The guy seemed bored, which made me angry. It made me clam up completely. He even knew that one day I would stop talking. Eventually I quit. My mum was upset. I live with my parents in Villejuif, it's a suburb just outside Paris. My mum's a nurse at the Fresnes prison. She loves her job. My dad is an art teacher at the secondary school. My parents are good people, that's not the problem.

What with you "fighting a battle against anger" and me "fighting against the urge to smash everything up", we should get along. And after listening to the other people's replies, I also thought what a super depressed bunch we are. Anyway, why are you angry? Honestly, you didn't come across as someone angry. You were the only one laughing with Esther. You were also the only one taking notes. When Esther asked me that killer question in her email, asking what battles I'm fighting, I didn't really think about it. I don't think I understood the question. Or rather, I just thought that it was a bit twisted. Then at the meeting, the answer hit me and I was suddenly talking about the urge to smash everything up. I even surprised myself. I have a good feeling about Esther, like I can trust her. Her smile calms me down. My answer just seemed to be waiting to pop out. And to be honest, I didn't think of you as elderly. You're not like any other old person I know.

Speak soon,
Samuel

John to Esther

Paris–New York, 6th February 2019

Hello Esther,
     Would you mind if we wrote to each other? I have chosen to write to Nicolas Esthover as well. You will know why when you receive a copy of my letter to him, as agreed, most probably when I return from New York. I'm going to make good use of my plane journeys. I'm the General Manager of Téléphonie et Digital and I've been flying frequently for work for a few years now. I'm mainly involved

in large restructuring projects and developing new international markets.

I wonder what made me decide to join your workshop. I mean it's not like I need to fill my schedule. When I read your ad, I remembered the letters my maternal grandmother, Manine, used to send me when I was at boarding school in Dijon. She would give me news from Paris, and especially liked to tell me about her games of rummy, which often ended up in a fist fight if she happened to be on José's team or if Linda was with Sylvie. She recounted these raucous evenings in lengthy reports several pages long which I delighted in reading: "You won't believe that right then and there he throws down his king of spades like he owns the place, the simpleton, as if to say, 'You're not playing with just anyone, you know'." "We can't do a thing about Sylvie, she's about as sharp as a spoon that one." My grandmother hated losing, even to me. In contrast to hers, my letters were rather dull. But I applied myself and really enjoyed writing to her. During my eight years as a boarder, I can honestly say that I can count on the fingers of one hand the weeks when I didn't get a letter. And I was always happy to see her when I returned to Paris twice a month. I never knew my maternal grandfather; he died before I was born. She didn't talk about him much, except to say that he was a brave and kind man, but the sort of person who would make three right turns to make a left. My grandmother enjoyed collecting such expressions. One day I will take the time to write them all down.

I was a model student. So for my parents, it was a given that I would go to France's top business school. And I did indeed get in. They were lucky with me and my siblings. None of us gave them a hard time. I was a docile young man. After graduating, I was recruited by a telecommunications company, then by another specializing in the latest technologies, and finally by Téléphonie et Digital. I was an expert in business plans, methodology, financial statements, payroll, and cost productivity. I quickly climbed the ladder.

I was on a permanent high. Just like when you gamble at the casino. I took chances and won every time. Arnaud and Pascal, the company founders, trusted me completely. Back then, the competition was not nearly as tough as it is today, and they poured a lot of money into the venture. They were very generous with me too. I had a good head for business and was probably born under a lucky star. Money excited me and success made me feel good; it gave me confidence. Women flattered me, and men respected me. I found the whole performance intoxicating. No matter how much I told myself each night in bed that I wasn't deluded and still had a sense of what money was worth, I was wrong. I dived in head first and wallowed in the mud with glee. The company quickly prospered. I was eager to satisfy their every whim and they gave me all the dirty work. They kept telling me how much they relied on me, and I was flattered. I used to say with fake modesty that "no one is indispensable", yet I did everything to make myself so. I needed it to feel alive. I was addicted to the adrenalin.

My grandmother would have hated the person I have become today. The years have gone by, yet I have missed something and don't know what. I am becoming increasingly indifferent to people and events, even if I pretend not to be. I would love to rediscover the joys of writing again. Maybe words will help me get better. Or at least make me realize what it is I want and understand my expectations.

What else is there left to tell you, Esther? I smoke and drink too much, the results of my medical checkups are not great. But I don't care. Or pretend I don't.

I look forward to hearing from you.
Best regards,
John Beaumont

At JFK airport, a driver is waiting for John to take him to the Hyatt. He doesn't have a minute to lose. Once inside his room, on the twentieth floor, he turns off the air-conditioning, dumps his suitcase, takes a shower and puts on a clean shirt while consulting his schedule on his laptop. He did jot down his meetings on the plane a few hours ago but has forgotten them already. He doesn't print stuff out any more.

Is it his age? A lack of motivation? Or is he just getting forgetful? Fifty-three isn't that old, he reassures himself. He looks out his window onto Central Park in all its splendour. It's time to go. John closes the bedroom door behind him. He would have loved to swim a few lengths of the pool. Outside, he lights a cigarette and locates his driver, who is waiting for him a few metres away.

For John Beaumont, all big cities look alike. Grey tarmac pavements, heavy traffic, signs indicating peak pollution levels and safety measures, the weather forecast, more and more digital billboards in the streets and shop windows, the roar of sirens, and trees wondering what the hell they are doing there. The inhabitants surge out of the underground stations and offices in clusters, headsets on, their eyes glued to their mobile phones stuck to the palm of their hands like an extension of their own flesh. They pour into buildings and stores. In the evening, they all go back in the opposite direction. John is not used to walking any more.

His driver follows him like a shadow. The car passes in front of the same logos, brand names and stores present in every other twenty-first-century concrete jungle. Tonight, his colleagues are taking him to a new restaurant, bragging how they managed to reserve a table there. Before his business trips, he used to promise himself that he would prolong his stay by forty-eight hours to sightsee and relax. He would wander around on his own, use public transport, casually stop off in cafés, you name it. To date, he has never done anything of the kind. When he was young, he was very resourceful. Nowadays, it's a different story. John Beaumont has become a loafer, someone who expects everything to be done for him.

He heads towards his car, then turns around and goes back into the hotel. He pulls an envelope out of his inner jacket pocket and hands it to the concierge. It's a letter for Esther Urbain, to be sent to France by priority mail.

Esther to John

Lille, 11th February 2019

Hello John,

You haven't portrayed yourself in a very flattering light. I know you're being frank, but aren't you painting rather too bleak a picture?

You hope that writing will help you put your emotions into words and combat your indifference. I indeed believe that writing can help us rebuild our lives. I trust that you will succeed.

Let's start with your childhood, if you don't mind. If you think I'm being intrusive, don't hesitate to tell me. I won't take offence, as I know I can be a bit blunt at times. This is one of the advantages (or disadvantages?) of written correspondence; you can't see the recipient's annoyance, boredom or anger.

Why did you go to a boarding school in Dijon? You don't mention your parents, is it because you were raised by your grandmother?

I don't know whether you are familiar with the Hauts-de-France area in the north of France? It's an interesting region with great appeal, which is making a big effort despite its economic difficulties to reinvent itself and embrace innovation. Lille is a very pleasant city to live in. The kindness and warmth of its residents is legendary. I love it here, especially in autumn and winter. Rain and fog suit it perfectly, unlike many other French regions. All it takes is a leaden grey sky and fog patches on the rooftops to give the city a wistful melancholic air that never fails to fascinate me. When I have time, I like to sit and read in a café there. In the summer, I make the most of the surrounding countryside, which is delightful and fortunately not very touristy. I hope this lasts! My Parisian friends are astonished when I tell them how beautiful this area is. But it's absolutely true.

I look forward to hearing from you soon.
Best regards,
Esther

P.S. I hope you understood my remarks about your first letter in the email I sent you. Let me know if you found it confusing. We must be careful to keep our conversation separate from what is strictly related to letter writing.

After the meeting at the Hoxton, I didn't go straight back to Lille. I slept at my cousin Raphael's place on Boulevard

Sébastopol. He is more than just my first cousin. He is my brother, my friend, my rock. We are both only children and were born just a few months apart. He lives in Paris, I live in Lille, but we have holidayed together many times with his parents and my father.

Raphael said he would be back late and left the keys under the mat. I promised myself that I wouldn't leave a mess, but within a few hours, the place looked like a whirlwind had hit it. I didn't realize this until the next morning, when he remarked on it, saying that he wouldn't have tolerated it from anyone else.

He prepared breakfast and went downstairs to buy the newspapers. I wanted to make him scrambled eggs, but he told me to sit down. He would take care of everything. I told him about my workshop. It's a shame no one writes letters nowadays. It's considered a waste of time. And these days, people want soundbites. However, I knew better than anyone, having corresponded with my father for twenty-two years, that we don't say the same things in writing as we do verbally. We use different words and expressions. We pay attention to our style. Our thoughts take different paths, which are more difficult to access, more complex, more unpredictable and more exhilarating too. When writing, we give ourselves away, we bare our soul, we take risks. The act of writing a letter, posting it and waiting for a reply adds value to the days. It also lends weight to the message in the envelope. The letter makes its journey to us in its own time.

I was disappointed not to have more students. Alice Panquerolles, who appeared interested on the phone, didn't come to the meeting or even bother to make her excuses. I tried to reach her, to no avail. The youngest member of the group sounded bored and I was afraid he would give up before he even started. I initially decided that each of them should write to two different people, but with only five students, this wouldn't work. I would have to become the sixth person. I was annoyed at myself for not having considered such an eventuality beforehand. What's more, I had expected everyone to be keen to write to me, given that I was the founder of the project.

"You have to be a little twisted to organize something like this, don't you?" I asked Raphael. He was evasive and just shrugged. But I knew what he was thinking. That I was potty and tiresome. He was the wise one of the family; the prize student. The one who could always be counted on, who didn't rock the boat, had a secure, well paid job in finance as well as a lovely fiancée, who was just like him. Not to mention an apartment that interior decoration magazines would jump at the chance to photograph. Oh, and let's not forget the Tesla . . .

He never understood why I needed other projects to focus on when my bookshop took up six days of my week. He loved to imitate me when I was grouchy. He would ruffle his hair, bite his lips, fiddle with his glasses: "How am I going to get through this? I'm so snowed under, I can't cope. If you knew how stressed I am, I've got anxiety . . . Do you have something to help me sleep?" I was sure he was worried about my latest endeavour and wondering what on earth I had got myself into yet again. I was wrong. Later on, he spoke about that day we spent together. He could see I had finally regained my former energy and enthusiasm. He hadn't said anything though, fearing that a remark, however slight, would serve as a reminder of my father's death. He had noticed how distracted and depressed I had become since my father's passing. He hated seeing me like that. He feared I would never be myself again: the person he had always known and adored. He, too, resented my father.

John to Nicolas

New York–Paris, 9th February 2019

Hello Nicolas,

I am a participant in Esther's writing workshop but couldn't make it to the meeting. I'm obliged to travel a lot for work so I plan to write while I'm in the air. At night. This is my favourite moment of the flight, when the lights go out signaling that it's time to sleep and the hubbub gives way to something resembling silence. No more conversations, no more trolleys in the aisle, no sounds of rustling food packaging or seat tables being opened or stowed away. I love this atmosphere, when the passengers doze off, curled up in their seats, buried under a blanket with an eye mask over their faces. Others wear headsets and put on film after film. I haven't watched anything in ages.

I chose you for two reasons. First, you are a chef at Camellia. I went there about ten years ago, with my children. The restaurant had just opened. The food was excellent. At least I thought it was. I remember that my children, who were teenagers at the time, wanted to go to Joe Allen's for a burger and fries. I vetoed that idea with the result that they sulked all evening. That was back when I wanted to teach them about good food. I soon gave up.

This brings me to the second reason. In her report, Esther told me that your wife is also in the workshop and that, for personal reasons, the two of you are writing to each other. You have succeeded in arousing my curiosity. This is good as I am striving to rid myself of my general indifference towards everything or almost everything; a tendency I am finding harder and harder to cope with. I won't give you any advice. It's not my style. I can't help you. Plus my personal life is in tatters so who am I to judge? As a husband, lover, father, I get *nil points*. If you have decided to write to your wife as part of a writing workshop, then you must care a lot about her. You have tenacity; I admire that. Hats off to you, from a guy who sat idly by as his wife and kids left him.

Do you mind if we correspond? We may not have much to say to each other as I doubt you are familiar with the telecommunications sector, but let's give it a shot. We can always talk about cooking, restaurants, hotels . . .

With kind regards,
John Beaumont

John is due to land at Roissy airport in two hours. He stashes away the envelope addressed to Nicolas. Writing brings back childhood memories of the sumptuous family flat on Avenue Victor Hugo in the expensive sixteenth district of Paris. He can recall the decor in detail: the patterns and colours of the carpets, the curtains, the paintings, the woodwork, the position of the furniture and the tiniest knick-knacks and ornaments, and where they were bought . . . He could have refurbished and redecorated that flat to look identical to how it was if he wanted. After his wife and children left, he still didn't sell the place. He lived there alone, rattling around in the huge, half-empty rooms. His friends advised him to move, but he stayed put, claiming it would be less traumatic for his children when they came see him every other weekend. In reality, he had been incapable of finding somewhere else to live, whether in the same district or elsewhere. He hadn't seen what difference it would make, apart from wasting his time. When his ex-wife heard that John had supposedly stayed put for Boris and Emma's sakes, she had laughed. She knew he wouldn't alter his work schedule for them and would only see them sporadically. With time, she had been proven right.

Three years ago, a friend had offered to sell John his flat. It was smaller than his but had a magnificent view of the Tuileries gardens near the Louvre. He had jumped at the chance. He didn't take a single piece of furniture from Avenue Victor Hugo with him. He had bought everything new, a symbol of his fresh start. Now he could happily spend the rest of his days on that balcony, never coming back down to earth, looking out at Paris and its monuments, its trees, the dust on windy days, the continuous flow of traffic along the Rue de Rivoli, the noisy bustling Place de la Concorde, and regulars strolling in the park.

Nicolas to John

Paris, 15th February 2019

Hi John,

It's funny, when I saw the picture Esther sent us, I liked your face. I thought you were a handsome man albeit a bit past his prime. No offence. I've got nothing against writing to you, but you're right, we don't have a lot in common. Your profession is so different to mine that I wouldn't know what questions to ask you even if I pretended to be interested. I hope you're not the sensitive type. I tend to call a spade a spade . . . But do feel free to tell me about your globetrotting.

Naturally it's better to have dinner at my place than at Joe Allen's, but I can understand your kids. It's much more fun when you're young to scoff down a scrumptious cheeseburger with fries in an American steakhouse than spend a boring evening in a Michelin starred restaurant eating gourmet dishes with ridiculous names you've never heard of.

Cooking was the only thing I ever wanted to do. My grandmother ran a brasserie in Bourg-en-Bresse, which my parents took over. There was no better place to enjoy the local delicacies: chicken liver loaf, frogs' legs, Bresse chicken *à la creme*, pike dumplings, Bresse buckwheat pancakes and so on. I followed the family tradition. Well, not exactly. After graduating from the Paul Bocuse Institute, I wanted to experiment and create something that was a bit more in keeping with the times than my parents' cuisine, although I was well aware of the expertise required to produce traditional dishes.

I would have gladly settled in Bourg-en-Bresse after my studies, but my wife, Juliette, wanted to live in Paris. I would have followed her to the end of the world. I met her in Madrid just after graduating—I was doing a six-month internship in the city. She was a tall, broad shouldered woman with endless legs, tanned skin, raven black hair and huge dark eyes. She had just passed her diploma to become a professional baker and was there celebrating with two friends. It didn't take long for me to fall in love with her. She was a brainy sort, believe me. Before specializing in baking and patisserie, she had studied literature at university in Normandy. When I met her, she was obsessed with Jean Echenoz and Philip Roth. It made for a slightly odd mix: that girl could chat away happily to you about ancient wheat varieties and then suddenly switch to talking about contemporary fiction. I bluffed my way through, pretending to be worldly, the guy who had been there done that, though deep down I lacked self-confidence. Today, she owns two bakeries. And not just any old bakeries, let me tell you. You should taste her bread, it's a work of art. Her farmhouse loaf with salted butter and homemade strawberry or clementine jam is to die for!

We lived together for sixteen years and now we're separated. I haven't got a clue whether it's temporary or permanent. Since the split, I've been battling with guilt and remorse. I find it hard to talk about it, even to my friends. One of these days, I'll tell you more. I feel tempted to open up to you about my private life, as yours is a mess too. What a happy thought. I can tell this is going to be a bundle of laughs . . . But what's the point of writing to each other if we just make small talk and don't get into the nitty gritty of things? We'd just bore the pants off each other.

Since Juliette left, my cooking has suffered. I can no longer work with anything round, smooth, creamy, sweet. Crème fraîche bores me, chocolate leaves me indifferent, red fruits exasperate me, and sugar repels me. I'm only inspired by acidic, sour flavours at the moment. I use and abuse the wonderful lemons from Sicily, as well as calamansi, tangelos, Buddha's Hand citrus fruits and grapefruits from Guyana. It must have a sharp tang and almost sting, like everything else in my life, I suppose. At this rate, my two Michelin stars won't last long. Juliette and I have a daughter. Her name is Adele. She is nine months old. I baked my favourite cake, a pavlova, to celebrate her birth. It's now on the menu. How old are your children? What do they get up to?

Nicolas

P.S. You're writing to me from up in the sky and I'm writing to you from my flat in Rue Oberkampf in east Paris. I live there with my daughter and my mother who helps me out with the little one. What a trio, eh?

Nicolas to Juliette

Paris, 11ᵗʰ February 2019

Juliette,

I still can't believe it. That you didn't even have the courage to tell me that you wanted to leave. That you had to hide behind your therapist to tell me! What's going on? Are you scared of me? Do I disgust you? You tricked me, made a fool of me and didn't give me any choice in the matter, and you know how I hate that. At that meeting with your therapist we were never going to discuss anything, because your mind was already made up. Why did she ask me what I thought about it, if she didn't want to hear my answer? When I said I didn't like the idea, neither of you said a word like you didn't care. I don't know whether you noticed but I didn't get angry. What's the point? I don't care if she reads this letter. That way she can say to you, "Mrs Esthover, it looks like you did the right thing in distancing yourself from your husband." I've been ostracized, like some wife beater who's been ordered to stay away from his spouse. And now we are reduced to writing to each other. Once again, do I have a choice? I want to help you, I'm on your side, but I need to understand what's going on. And I don't.

N.

Juliette to Nicolas

Malakoff, 14th February 2019

Hello Nicolas,

You're right, it was cowardly of me. My anxiety attacks came back, just a few days after I got home. I didn't want you to notice or see me in this state again. I can imagine how I look when it happens; like a complete psycho. When I left the maternity unit I thought I was getting better. Not that I was cured, but that the attacks were over. But I was mistaken. I went under again. It only took a few days for me to totally fall apart. Adele's crying drove me insane, just as it had before I was hospitalized. I was unable to look after her, it was overwhelming me. I was afraid of hurting her, and my belief that I was a rubbish mother resurfaced. "It's better that she doesn't have a mother at all than a mother like me", I would tell myself over and over again. I panicked as soon as you left for work.

Fear of falling asleep, fear of waking up. Do you know what that feels like? No. It all came back, so fast. As if the monster was simply lying dormant inside me, just long enough to regain its strength and attack me even more ferociously. My stays at the hospital and the maternity ward didn't help at all. I couldn't have found the words to explain it all to you. What I feared more than anything was that weary look on your face.

Juliette

Jean to Juliette

Verjus-sur-Saône, 12th February

Hello Juliette,

I am Jean, we met at the workshop. We could try to write to each other, what do you think? I admit, I'm a little late in getting started. After writing to young Samuel, I waited in vain for one of you to contact me. I wondered (I'm being candid here) if it was due to my age. What does this old woman want from us? To talk about her past, her illnesses, her solitude? That's probably what you thought, isn't it? And also why did I have that stupid grin on my face? It's daft really but I was just nervous.

I love writing letters and don't get the chance any more. I'm glad to be able to do it again. I correspond with my friends who live elsewhere, like everyone else, by phone or email. That's how it is nowadays, isn't it? I wish it were otherwise. Esther is right, we don't confide in each other in the same way verbally as when writing. In an email, we deal with the most urgent things, we don't bother about style. Our handwriting says something about us too. As does our writing paper. What I like best about written correspondence is the fact that time takes its time. And that the letter has to travel to its destination. Plus the numerous questions we ask ourselves like "When will she read it?", "When will she reply?", "Is it a nice letter?", "Have I convinced her?" or "Have I used the right words?" Esther could have named her workshop "A tribute to patience and the art of slowing down".

For the past twelve years, I have been living in the country, just over eighteen miles away from Lyon. Verjus was a very pretty village when I first moved there. That was before the housing developments slowly but surely gnawed away at it with their white plastered Lego cubes, their straw-coloured shutters and tired gardens. I used to live in Lyon, on the peninsula. I was a piano teacher until polyarthritis forced me to retire. I battled against the disease and tried to ignore it. But it was mightier than me and one day it got the better of me and forced me to stop. I still play for myself, when my fingers obey me. I really loved my job. After graduating from the music academy, I could have been a concert pianist, but I preferred to teach piano at home. My doorbell would ring at all times of the day. I loved teaching children most of all. It was sheer joy to hear the piano keys jumping, bouncing, stumbling, stammering . . . That's how I wanted it to be. When I felt that my little students needed motivating, I would give them a break and play something for them. Sometimes I would tell them stories. Playing the piano is not just about knowing how to read sheet music.

You also learn the history of classical music and about the composers' lives. Some parents said I wasn't strict enough. I agreed with them, but that was my style and they could take it or leave it. I hated it when my students gave up playing, when they became teenagers or went to university. It felt like a personal failure of sorts.

Hadrian died nine years ago. From a heart attack. Fifty-nine is too young to die. He was a good man. He gave me a good life. I tried to live up to his expectations. I was blessed to have met him.

I'm probably boring you to death with my rabbiting on. You've got better things to do. Maybe you only want to write to your husband? During the meeting, I noticed how far apart from each other you sat. I guessed things couldn't be going too well between you. I don't know you. That was the first time I'd seen you. You looked tired. I don't want to pry, but I'm here if you ever need to talk. Sometimes it's easier to talk to someone you don't know.

Very best wishes,
Jean

P.S. It may not be immediately obvious, but I'm fighting a constant battle with anger. I am revolted by the way in which we are destroying the countryside and ill-treating animals.

Jean struggled in her attempt to write to Juliette. Her first three drafts ended up in the bin. She knows how carried away she can get and how outspoken she can be. She doesn't want to offend Juliette or appear intrusive, but she can't pretend she didn't notice how sad the woman looked. Juliette is pretty but has let herself go. Her long black hair tumbling halfway down her back was dull and lifeless. Her nails were bitten to the quick, her sweater was shapeless, and her corduroy slacks were too big for her. Her athletic body, wide shoulders and long legs exude strength and confidence, but appearances can be deceptive. Jean recognizes this fragile, abandoned and tormented look. She has seen it many times before among the adults she has taught. Most of them women. She knows how to spot them now, after years of experience. There are certain tell-tale signs. Hands trembling on the keyboard, shoulders hunched, irregular and rapid breathing, a forced smile, an absent gaze, and the sad tunes they chose to play. Jean's patience, her soft, reassuring voice, and her naturally spontaneous and joyful disposition put them at ease and some even confided in her. She has heard it all: nightmarish divorces, adultery, problem children, uncommunicative teenagers, the first time they were hit by their husband, then the second time, followed by his promises to repent, unemployment, the feeling of betrayal when placing elderly parents in a home . . .

Jean can tell Juliette is struggling with life.

Juliette to Jean

Malakoff, 16th February

Jean,

You said you did your best to live up to your husband's expectations. You wouldn't have mentioned this if you hadn't succeeded. That's more than can be said for me! I failed miserably. It was all too overwhelming, and I sank all the way back down again. Now I don't know how to get back up or if I even have the courage or will to do so. Don't judge me please.

I'm a baker. I own two bakeries: one in Paris in the eleventh district, and one in the Paris suburb of Malakoff. I work with traditional flours, favouring slow kneading and long baking times. I supply Michelin starred chefs with special breads. My bestsellers are my baguettes with ginger and my "black bread"— baguettes made with vegetable carbon—as well as my rye bread. I met Nicolas in Madrid, at a youth hostel. We had both just finished our studies. I loved him as soon as I saw him, I totally and utterly loved everything about him. There was something irresistible about this sturdily built young man, with his blue eyes and long curly hair, who stood over six feet tall. How can I put it? He oozed innocence, an innocence that I envied. He knew exactly what he was going to do with his life: cook. And he knew he would succeed. That's how he put it, candidly without any pretentiousness. His honesty made me want to smile. I leant on his strength of character and self-confidence for years. "It's you," he told me, so sure of himself, the first morning after the first night. "It's me what?" I replied stupidly. "You're the one. The woman I love." I should have run, but I stayed. What more could I want than to be wrapped in his embrace? We returned to France, to Bourg-en-Bresse where he grew up. His parents owned an excellent brasserie in the town centre. They welcomed me with open arms and were nice, kind people, but the family atmosphere was suffocating. I wanted to live in Paris, and make it my new home. I wanted to experience something different from Trouville, the small seaside town where I grew up. Nicolas was willing to try it, so six months later, we moved into a studio flat in the east of Paris. He found a job at a Michelin starred restaurant called L'Astrance, while I was recruited by Landemaine, a reputable bakery and patisserie. In our line of work, there's no shortage of jobs.

But in the capital, we weren't able to save as much as we had hoped. Luckily, five years later, his parents lent us some money, enabling Nicolas to open his own restaurant, his very first, on Rue Oberkampf. It was a tiny little place and could just about seat twelve people. After a lick of paint, a new kitchen, tables and chairs bought at the local flea market plus Nicolas' culinary talents, the restaurant took off. It was always fully booked and the press and food critics started to take an interest. Nicholas was soon included in various distinguished gourmet food guides.

Around this time, I took over the lease of a cheap and cheerful bakery in Malakoff. I can hardly begin to describe the thrill, Jean, or the excitement I felt, the day I opened the doors of my very own bakery and welcomed my very first customers! I'll never forget those dazzling few seconds as long as I live. When I close my eyes, I can still feel that adrenalin rush, as if it hasn't yet left me for good. Like the wind when it brushes against your face. Opening a bakery is more than just making and selling bread and pastries. The bakery is the focal point of the village or town. The place that unites business people and the unemployed, career women and stay-at-home mums and dads, the one place virtually everyone stops by daily. It's also where you send your child to run his or her very first errand. Along with the bistro, the bakery is the very heart of the town. A necessary and happy place. When I took my diploma, I was surprised to see that many students had chosen baking as a plan B. For me it was by far my first choice.

To get to my bakery, I would leave home on my moped in the middle of the night. The noise of the rubbish lorries followed me through the sleepy Parisian streets, along the deserted pavements where rats were king for a few hours. I remember how I felt in the middle of winter, shivering in the icy rain, exhausted from lack of sleep but eager to get to my beloved bakery, come what may. "I just love masochists," joked Nicolas. He always got home late in the evening. It was a strange life for a young couple. We would pass each other like ships in the night. We were told: "You won't last long at this rate". We didn't see what the problem was and quite right too. We wanted to enjoy life, just the two of us and get our careers established before having children. The time went by in a blur and one day I woke up pregnant at thirty-eight years old. Our daughter, Adele, was born. Nothing was ever the same again. I'm not able to talk about it yet. I can only say that I felt like I was being suffocated, rather like being buried alive. Since then, I have been fighting against the sensation of being swallowed up. My daughter is nine months old.

I'm only really happy when I've got my hands in flour, when I can feel the pulsing heat of the ovens, smell the freshly baked bread, and observe my loaves swelling and rising. My latest bread is called La Belle Brune. It's made with stout and raisins, and smells of toasted sesame seeds. Other specialties include my tasty "crispy chocolate" cakes with dulce de leche, and my "Sunday brioche" flavoured with honey and cocoa from Chuao. Nicolas and I used to spend entire evenings discussing culinary creations, restaurants, grocery stores, and names for his dishes and my cakes and breads. Do you like big round farmhouse loaves of bread with a golden crunchy crust, a pearly crumb and that just out of the oven toasted smell?

Juliette

IN THE BEGINNING

Jean to Juliette

Verjus-sur-Saône, 20th February 2019

Hello Juliette,

Thanks to you, I experienced a rare pleasure this morning. Upon checking my letterbox, what did I find among the unpleasant bills and monotonous bumf but a handwritten envelope. This unusual discovery instantly ignited my curiosity.

I found your letter very moving. You use the past tense when talking about your happy times with Nicolas. However, I notice you talk about your husband with a lot of affection. What on earth happened? From your letter, everything points to you being a rock-solid couple. As I said in my letter to you, Hadrian was the great love of my life. I was still at music school when I met him at a party in Paris. I remember the flat in Montmartre. It was huge and looked out onto the Sacré-Coeur. Beatrice, one of my best friends, insisted on taking me along. Hadrian was one of several medical students celebrating their graduation that evening. "You'll see," she warned me, "medical students are the biggest party animals out there." And I wasn't disappointed. At five o'clock in the morning, Hadrian and I ended up at Pied de Cochon, a restaurant that basically never closes. He was off to Freetown in Sierra Leone a few days later. He had visited the country with his parents when he was a teenager and had always dreamed of going back. He planned to practise there as a physician for a while, before returning to France. He had no idea exactly how long he would be gone. He wanted to give himself some leeway. We were inseparable right up until his departure. I'm not sure that our time together would have been so intense had we not been conscious every second of his leaving, like a ticking bomb. We had no time to lose. I took him to the airport and watched his plane take off. I was pleased for him, and yet resigned to never seeing him again. I didn't think for a second that he would write to me. He wrote as soon as he arrived. Then his letters got more and more frequent during his fourteen months away. It was hard to resist such a funny and lovable man.

When he returned, I went to pick him up at the airport. When I saw him through the window, I found him so handsome that I almost got cold feet. He was tanned and wearing a colourful African shirt and wooden-beaded necklaces. His shoulder-length hair had golden highlights from the sun. The experience had boosted his confidence.

I still like to read his letters today. They serve as a reminder of how much we loved each other. It makes me sad, though it's not unpleasant. It's that damn thing called nostalgia. It comes and goes in waves. We soon moved to Lyon because we didn't particularly want to live in Paris. He set up his practice in the Croix-Rousse district. He was a very popular and reliable doctor. He did voluntary work two and a half days a week in an emergency shelter for homeless men. He supported his patients and even acted as a social worker when circumstances required it. He helped them deal with red tape, indifference, and contempt. He never got angry, never gave up, and almost always eventually obtained what he had promised them.

Every summer, we travelled to a different far-flung destination. This was our only holiday of the year. We went to Africa many times: Mozambique, Sierra Leone, the Ivory Coast. I suspected he wanted to visit these remote areas with a view to doing voluntary medical work there. He was hardly interested in the landscapes.

Over the years, more and more of our friends divorced. Each new split saddened us. Hadrian and I were like two survivors in a battlefield of ruins. We hadn't experienced betrayal, boredom, anger, jealousy. Why us? What did we have that they didn't? Nothing. To top it all, we didn't want children, which baffled our relatives. We were happy on our own. We were comfortable with it, even if it was a touchy subject, especially for me. A woman who doesn't want children is seen by others as abnormal, incomplete, and obviously traumatized and/or neurotic. I loved spending my days with children; so why didn't I want my own? I saw no connection between teaching piano and motherhood. I failed to convince many people of this, however. There were also those who avoided the subject, convinced that one of us was infertile. Has society changed its view of women who don't want children? I don't think so . . .

I was thirty-seven years old when I fell pregnant. It was an accident. We weren't sure whether to keep the baby. It was my age that finally convinced us. We probably wouldn't have another chance. Our daughter, Aurélie, was born. She brought us much happiness. She has just turned thirty.

Hadrian had a heart attack ten years ago in Tanzania while we were on holiday. The day before he died, we were walking in the Lushoto mountains. He turned to me, smiled and said, "I haven't been feeling very well all morning. I'll ask the guide if he can take me to the hospital tomorrow." I suggested that he go right away. "Why wait?" I insisted. The pain in his shoulder and his shortness of breath were signs that something was wrong. He laughed it off and told me to stop worrying. "Who's the doctor here? It's all right, it's just exhaustion, that's all. I'll go to bed early and we'll take our time and go after breakfast." He was agitated all night. We got up at dawn. He was as white as a sheet. I spent about twenty minutes in the bathroom opposite our chalet. Then I went straight to the kitchen on the other side of the complex to pick up our breakfast tray. I was trying my best to be quick. I came back to find Hadrian dead at the foot of the bed. So now you see, dear Juliette, life sometimes takes an unexpected turn. How utterly and preposterously absurd it can be. Maybe you have already experienced this madness yourself. If you only knew how I regretted letting him make that choice.

Hadrian is buried in the village cemetery, but I don't ever go. What's the point? I avoid having to pass it even. His grave must be in a terrible state, but I don't care. I'd rather talk to him here at home. I mean, it's no sillier than standing in front of a gravestone. The echoing silence is the same. The corpse encased in a coffin, rotting and decaying, only to become dust, is no longer him.

You can see how open I have been with you. And, believe me, it's not easy. Now it's your turn: try telling me about what's worrying you.

Kind regards,
Jean

Juliette to Jean

Malakoff, 24th February 2019

Hi Jean,

Do you know what postpartum depression is? It affects women who have just had a baby. Men can suffer from it too, but it's uncommon. It's one difficulty of being a mother, and a dark side of motherhood that isn't talked about enough. This is the misfortune that hit me when I gave birth to my daughter. I am not yet able to talk to you about it I'm afraid. If I attempt to remember that sequence of events and relate them in chronological order, retracing my long descent into hell, I risk rekindling my trauma. On the other hand, I could try to talk to you about the condition objectively, telling the story not so much from my perspective but on behalf of all the women who suffer from it, even if our experiences differ. Maybe later on I'll be able to write about what happened to me. If I manage to do so, I'll have succeeded in overcoming the tremendous shame I still feel about it. It will be a huge victory for me, but I'm not ready yet.

Jean, you should know that before suffering from it I would have been incapable of telling you what postpartum depression was. The vast majority of women who have just given birth are in a state of overwhelming exhaustion and vulnerability, which can cause unhealed wounds and unanswered questions to resurface. Not to mention unresolved childhood trauma and unpleasant memories. A difficult pregnancy, a complicated delivery, a painful episiotomy, an emergency C-section, an inability to breastfeed, unsympathetic midwives and nurses who don't meet our expectations, and tensions within the family all heighten new mothers' feelings of inadequacy and are possible triggers for PPD. In the case of particularly fragile mothers, these will precede the resulting nervous breakdown, which is often initially diagnosed simply as fatigue, lack of sleep or baby blues.

Once home, sufferers of PPD feel incompetent and are petrified of doing the wrong thing with their baby. They believe they lack the necessary tools. In panic, they

wonder why they don't have the maternal instinct that has
been drummed into them since birth. We women grow up
with an iron-clad dogma: there is no greater happiness
than having a child. If you knew how angry this makes
me! Then, in desperation, these new mothers conceal their
suffering. For them, congratulatory visits from family and
friends who are ecstatic about the baby are a real ordeal.
They are at odds with themselves, trying to put on a brave
face. If they start to cry, they are urged to rest, and their
behaviour is put down to baby blues, considered to be a
natural and fleeting phenomenon with no lasting effects.
All victims of postpartum depression experience shame
and guilt. They hear their own distress in their baby's cries,
a cry for help that they cannot answer. It reflects a mon-
strous image of themselves. Their solitude is real. When
they give birth, they find themselves alone with their child,
unable to meet his or her needs, unable to offer tenderness or love. The birth opens up a Pandora's box that they
didn't know existed. The days go by, their distress increas-
es, they feel useless, they sink into despair and end up
losing their grip. Sometimes they take a dislike to this little
being who plagues their days and nights. And I'm not exaggerating here. How many of these women have felt the
furious and insane urge to throw their baby out of the window, or smother him or her with a pillow? Have imagined
themselves doing it? I know I have. It's impossible for
them to be mothers. By becoming mothers, they no longer
exist. It's either their child or them. "I'm the eggshell that
was smashed to pieces to release the chick," said one of
the women on the maternity ward where I'm treated. This
describes perfectly what they all feel, convinced that they
are not up to the task. Which is true, they are not. And yet,
without their baby they are not themselves either, since
they can't put the clock back to the time before they were

pregnant. Women suffering from postnatal depression all say the same thing: it's a descent into hell.

Juliette

When she's not in the maternity unit, Juliette tries her hardest, as advised, to "live in the moment". Antidepressants and tranquilizers soothe her and keep the pain at bay. Just writing about postpartum depression was enough to trigger her low mood again. It was a mistake to think she could write about it on behalf of all sufferers and protect herself. Her head is spinning, she panics and is about to go delirious. If only she hadn't become pregnant, and hadn't had her daughter, everything would go back to how it was before the birth, which ruined everything. Yet, she loves her baby, and doesn't want to hurt her. It's poor innocent little Adele who needs protecting, and who has the right to happiness. Juliette is the monster. She curls up in the foetal position on her bed. She breathes slowly and regularly. Her pills are right there beside her to send her to sleep.

Jean to Samuel

Verjus-sur-Saône, 21st February 2019

Dear Samuel,

If you like to write on paper napkins, don't let me stop you. Your writing is easy to read anyway. Taking part in a writing workshop rather than temping at a supermarket shows that you have gumption. How old are you, Samuel? I gather that you're not in further education or working. Do you not get bored? When I was a child, I used to spend the long summer holidays with my parents in Corrèze, where they had a small holiday home. We would spend four weeks there, just the three of us, bang in the middle of the countryside. You can't imagine how bl★★★★ fed up I was! Fortunately, I had music. I was an only child, I didn't have any friends in the area, except for my first cousin who lived on the other side of the village.

She filled her days with whatever she could find, be it pencils, felt tips, beads, earth, pieces of tile . . . I admired her. She was talented with her hands. In comparison, I was a real butterfingers. I wanted her to admire me too, and all I had was the piano. So when she came to my house, I would play for her. It was a waste of time though as she usually left the room after a few minutes, slamming the door behind her. Outside, she climbed trees with the agility of a monkey and if we played hide-and-seek, she always won. She hid in nooks and crannies where I was afraid to venture. She didn't need me to have fun and let me know it. I wanted to excel at something to impress her but she wouldn't play along. One day, boredom got the better of me and I decided to go to the village library and start reading. I chose *Bel-Ami* by Guy de Maupassant. It was literally love at first sight.

If someone had told me that one day I would live in the country, I wouldn't have believed them. I live in a house in the middle of a vineyard. I wish I could write "lost among the grapevines", but it wouldn't be credible given that I'm surrounded by housing estates! Hadrian, my husband, was a doctor. After we graduated in Paris, I followed him to Lyon, where he opened a GP practice in the Croix-Rousse district. For years, I gave my students piano lessons from our home. Then Hadrian wanted to move to the country, where there was a shortage of doctors (as is still the case today). I must admit I was dreading moving there but it turned out to be a blessing in disguise as we now owned meadows where we could keep animals. My dream come true. We settled in Verjus, a village of just 1,300 inhabitants. The locals were delighted to hear a general practitioner was opening a surgery there, and the relief in their faces was enough to reassure me we had made the right decision. I still journeyed to Lyon several times a week to give lessons at people's homes and at the music academy. I gave lessons in the village too.

My husband passed away ten years ago. He was fifty-nine years old. That's young to die. I am sixty-seven. You asked me why I spoke of anger. Well, because I like fighting battles. That's what gets me out of bed in the morning. Oh, don't get me wrong, my battles are miniscule in the big scheme of things and I can count my victories on one hand. However, fighting for a cause makes me feel alive and—how can I say this without sounding either utopian or naive?—*involved* in the world around me. I do understand those who find me tiresome, but in fairness, I'm what you call a sensitive female warrior. I am devoted to animals. I want them to be respected and given their rightful place in society. Do you ever watch animal documentaries, Samuel? There are some extraordinary ones on the telly. All animals, from the smallest to the largest, possess their own unique intelligence and abilities, and extraordinary intuition. I'm not going to list all the misfortunes that man has inflicted on them here. And I'm equally wary of extremists who find them more virtuous than humans. But let's face it, when it comes to cruelty towards animals, and exploiting them in any way possible, there is no end to our resources and imagination. This saddens and depresses me. Just yesterday, I discovered the existence of the Blood Festival in Peru. Bulls have to endure being pecked by condors whose legs are sewn into the flesh of the bulls' backs. As the condors try to free themselves, they perform a kind of excruciating rodeo. The condor makes the bull suffer, and the bull causes the condor great suffering in turn. This is just one ritual among thousands in the realm of cruelty that humans like to inflict on animals. We must protect our animals and respect nature, otherwise we'll pay a heavy price for it one day.

I've also campaigned against intensive farming, animal shows, glue-trap hunting, and the practice of slaughtering animals without pre-stunning. I sign petitions, I help grassroots associations contact policy-makers, and I meet with politicians and the heads of organizations and foundations in an attempt to raise their awareness of causes that concern them directly. In the summer, I help in local animal shelters for abandoned pets. It's hard to stay motivated after all these years, given that most of the time my efforts end in failure. And then I pull off a small victory and wham! I regain the momentum I need to start fighting all over again.

I'll tell you about my animals if you like. Do you have any?

I am also fighting against the housing developments that are springing up willy nilly in my area. I'm well aware that the planet can't cope with the increasing population, that we need to build more homes and that each of us must have a roof over our heads. This is the excuse we use to destroy our landscapes and encroach a little more on nature every day. So be it. We have no choice. But why sacrifice aesthetics? And line up identical concrete blocks that resemble Legoland? They retort that it's easy for me to say that, with my pretty little stone house. "Ah, those city dwellers!" they think. Rubbish, you can build something nice for not much more. Don't take me for a simpleton. Some architects and/or developers involve the future owners upstream at the design stage. They have a say in the exterior and interior of the flats, the layout of the rooms, the decoration . . . There are even shared facilities such as a laundry, a guest flat, and a room for meetings and parties. I'm getting carried away, I'm ranting again . . . sorry, Samuel.

Now, tell me why you're fighting against the urge to smash everything up?

Best wishes,
Jean

Samuel to Jean

1st March

Hello Jean,
I actually quite like writing on paper napkins, and since you don't mind I'll carry on. My mum says the same as you (except she says it angrily): "Don't you get bored doing nothing?" When my brother was in hospital and I used to keep him company in the afternoons, the time dragged. I didn't dare play on my phone. I was supposed to talk to him, but didn't know what to say. I think he understood and found it amusing. Julian was three years older than me. He had cancer for a long time. He died on 25th October 2017, at the age of twenty-one. Well almost. He would have been twenty-one the week after. I realized not long ago that I don't know how long he was ill for. It seemed like he was ill forever, like I had only ever known him that way, but I could be wrong. One cancer gave way to another. Maybe he was born healthy, a normal little boy like the others. I started wondering about all this after his death. I never thought about it before. For me, it was as if he had always been ill and would be ill all his life. I didn't think he would ever get better, nor did I think he would die. I can't talk about it with my parents. We don't mention him any more, it's become taboo. I wonder how we got to this point. In a way though, it's easier like this. I don't know

how to deal with my mum's grief. I have no way of con-
soling her. Nothing I can say or do helps, which makes me
feel even more of a shit towards her. I hear her crying in
their room, before my dad goes to bed. They used to go
to bed at the same time. She tries not to make any noise,
but I can hear her. Our walls are like cardboard. I recognize the sound of sobs choking and fading into a pillow.
I grew up with it. At times it makes me want to smash up
everything in sight, and sometimes it makes me want to
cry. Since Julian died, my mum's nightly crying fits have
become second nature to her. My dad, on the other hand,
has become withdrawn. He takes medication to cope.
My parents hardly talk to each other. I try to remember
how they were before Julian's death. In fact, that's all they
talked about even then. The latest chemo sessions, the
new treatment plan, which one of them would be free to
take him to his physiotherapist, and for his next MRI . . .
Julian took up all the space between my parents and me,
and now I can see that he took up all the space between
my mum and dad too.

My dad hasn't been able to paint since my brother's
death. And I haven't been able to cry. It's as if everything
stopped the day my parents told me it was the end. I knew
beforehand that there would be no one to console me, I
certainly didn't want to add to my parents' grief. All three
of us did the same. We each cried on our own, to spare
each other. I went into the forest to scream. Nothing came
out. One night I drank myself stupid, but I couldn't even
throw up. I had a hangover for two days. My body is like
a fortress, I'm constantly on the lookout and I'm so tense
that I hurt everywhere. I feel like if I let go, I could do
something stupid, and smash everything up. I shouldn't be
telling you this, it's not your problem, but you asked me
why I had this urge.

No, I don't have any pets. I would love a dog. What sort of pets do you have? What did your husband die of? I never want to have children.

You asked me what I do all day. It depends. I see my mate, Ben, and we watch *Game of Thrones* together, but right now he's working in a restaurant so we hardly see each other. I geek around a lot, I do errands for my mum, I help her out when she asks me. I don't read. I watch TV shows. I got hooked on that series, *Spiral*, but that was a long time ago. When my dad brings back the local newspaper, I take a look. To be honest, I don't really like reading. I can't see myself in a bookshop or a library; those kinds of places intimidate me. I wouldn't know what to do with myself, or what to choose.

Studying isn't my thing either. I was lousy at school anyway. When Julian died, it didn't get any better. I got expelled in Year Eleven. My mum tried to enrol me in a private secondary school, but I asked her to get off my back until the end of the year. She agreed. Not that she gave a toss anyway. When my parents broached the subject again, I just refused and told them no more school. I decided to find myself a training course instead. But the truth is, I haven't even started looking. It's been a year and a half and nothing's changed.

Samuel

John to Nicolas

Brussels–Paris, 22nd February 2019

Hi Nicolas,

You're not alone. When my wife left, I couldn't bring myself to talk about it. I couldn't tell anyone that I didn't feel anything. Not happy, not sad, not relieved. Nothing.

Masha is Russian. She grew up in Moscow. I met her during a series of conferences in Paris on big data technologies and their impact on society. She was speaking as the manager of a large Russian cosmetics chain. We began dating and after a few trips back and forth between Paris and Moscow, she moved in with me. Masha was a brilliant and ambitious woman—she still is. I need to stress this because the cliché of the Eastern European woman marrying a rich European for his money makes my hair stand on end. It would be grotesque to apply it to us; we were in love. She took intensive French classes and got a new management position, still in the cosmetics industry.

Six months after we met, she told me she wanted a baby. I couldn't see the rush. We had plenty of time—our whole lives ahead of us. I was in love. I wanted to enjoy our time together, just the two of us. Why this sudden urge? The idea of having a baby came as a blow to me. It's gross of me, but I prayed that she wouldn't get pregnant. But she did, three months later. After Boris was born, I became the third wheel. It signaled the end of my marital bliss. I always felt in the way. It wasn't Masha's fault. I felt like I'd been struck down in my prime. Emma was born two years later. I didn't change anything in my life just because I became a father. On the contrary, I sought refuge in my work.

One day Macha fell in love with someone else. I felt no pain, no jealousy, no joy, no anger, no relief, no blow to my ego. Boris was eleven years old when we separated, and Emma was nine. My wife and children had left me. But I remained unruffled, faithful to my routine of meetings, business lunches, and calls across different time zones; the daily grind that governed my weeks. I'm just passing through, don't mind me . . .

We managed to have a painless divorce. No battles over money, custody or the flat. I gave her what she wanted and what I thought was fair. She got remarried a few years later to an up-and-coming French painter who was beginning to be noticed in arty circles. She didn't leave me for him, by the way. As for my children, I have almost no contact with them. It's not their fault. I'm the only one to blame.

Speak to you soon,
John

Nicolas to John

Paris, 4th March 2019

Hey John!

You need to step up man! Life is too short for moping around. What's with the jaded tone? Are you always like this? I hope not. And that victim attitude you seem to be wallowing in? So it's all your fault, concerning your wife and children? For pity's sake stop acting so hard done by. Look, you've got a great career. I've got no desire to correspond with someone so depressing. I don't need it, believe me, because when it comes to troubles, I've had my fair share!

You need a lot of energy and belief in what you're doing to motivate your staff, right? I googled you and came across a rather flattering picture in the press: steely eyes, strong jawline, and classy black suit, wow! Travelling doesn't seem to float your boat any more . . . Could you not delegate and put your anchor down in Paris or elsewhere? Personally, if I don't turn up at my restaurant every day with a big smile on my face and a fighting spirit, ready to give it my best shot, my staff and customers would soon make me pay. Must be the same for you.

You say you have "almost no contact" with your children. Is that true? Why?

It must be cool living on Rue de Rivoli, even if it is noisy. Does your flat actually have a view over the Tuileries gardens?

Today I'm paying the price for yesterday. We were really short staffed in the kitchen and when it's like that, the pressure is horrendous. But we have to get it right, send it all out on time. I just about coped but I can't perform miracles. When it's like this I'm in firefighting mode, meaning I deal with the most urgent things first. This isn't me though, I hate it, I want every dish I send out to be perfect, no exceptions. When you're a chef, you learn to live with stress. The heat is really on in the lunch and dinner rushes. Hopefully as I get older, I'll learn to handle it better.

Do you cook, John? I know you do, Esther, we talked about it together. On that subject, Esther (sorry, John, to go off at a tangent for a moment), I've been reading up on culinary specialties from northern France and I'm thinking of trying some stews, maybe Waterzoï or the Carbonade version with beef and beer. Waffles too maybe when I'm back on sugar again.

John, I must tell you about my wife and daughter. Since Adele was born, I no longer know what planet I'm on. I've discovered the immense joys of fatherhood. Shame that you missed out on it. It was the opposite for my wife, Juliette. She hated being pregnant. She had nightmares, thought she was fat and ugly, couldn't stand waddling around slowly, like a duck, and complained nonstop. It was a real nuisance for her. I was on the receiving end of her ill humour; no matter what I did or said. Juliette had never been capricious or temperamental before. I couldn't understand why she had changed, but I wasn't overly worried, just surprised, and annoyed. I put it down to the pregnancy. So I decided to grin and bear it. I thought everything would get better when the baby arrived. I got it all wrong. There was a hint of cowardice in my denial. A *je ne sais quoi* of cowardice, you might say. Wouldn't it be nice to invent a dish called a "*Je ne sais quoi*"? It sounds fleeting and mysterious doesn't it? When she came out of the maternity clinic, Juliette would burst into tears at the drop of a hat. I remember wondering to myself whether it was that odd thing they call the baby blues. If it was, then it's lasting a heck of a long time . . . Looking after Adele proved to be a real ordeal for Juliette. She gave her the bottle, changed her nappy, held her for five minutes at set times, but she wasn't really there. She was on automatic pilot. I often came home from the restaurant to find Juliette in our room with the door closed, lying on the bed with her eyes wide open. Adele would be crying in her crib, but Juliette couldn't hear her. Or didn't want to hear her. She couldn't tell me what was wrong either. I was totally lost. Everything I loved about my wife, her cheerfulness, her energy, had evaporated. I was confused. I let the days pass, hoping she would get better. At the restaurant, I was fraught and on edge. The more time went by, the more I told myself that it was madness to leave them on their own. I was wary of Juliette's reactions and what might happen. Eventually, I gave up. I put my head in the sand, refusing to acknowledge that there was a major problem. I spent my days toing and froing between home and the restaurant. Looking back, I had several near misses on my moped. I wanted Juliette to talk to me but couldn't get anywhere with her. In all honesty, she was pissing me off big time.

I've got a real problem now: I can't erase the images of Juliette during that period. She looked like a woman who was completely off her head, with a crazed look in her eyes. She was jealous of Adele. Can you imagine? Jealous of her own daughter! I didn't even know that was possible. I wish I could erase this sad memory of her. Some days, I wanted to kick her out of bed, and force her to move. I hated the person I was then, powerless to help and reassure her. I have since learnt that depression is an illness that I don't understand. But I still don't have much sympathy for those who suffer from it. I feel like telling them to pull themselves together, stop complaining and get moving! Our time on this earth is limited, no point wasting it. Yes, I know I'm way off the mark. But I was feeling completely disorientated, you know? And when that happens, I can act like a real idiot. I clam up and sulk, doing my darndest to put up a front.

My beloved Juliette whom I thought I knew inside out, who had been my lover, my wife, my friend, had gone. Patience is not my forte. I admit I was hard on her. Though to be fair, I was on my knees. She would get up at set times to take care of Adele, then go back to bed or sit on the couch with a magazine. The day I realized she wasn't reading a single line and was just staring at a dot on the page, I panicked. I told her to make an appointment with our doctor. I thought she would get on her high horse and refuse, but she agreed right away, as if she'd been waiting for my approval. The fool prescribed vitamins and rest, reassuring her she would wake up one morning and her baby blues would be gone. It was all a bad joke! Because of him, we lost two months. Her condition deteriorated. In actual fact, she had postpartum depression. It was the first time I had heard of this illness. And now we're in for the long haul. She was admitted to a psychiatric hospital, before being transferred to a maternity unit. Then she came home, and shortly after, she left me and Adele. Now we are writing to each other via the workshop. My mother has moved in to help me and Adele, as my hours are too unsocial to hire a nanny.

If someone had told me that one day I would tell all this to a guy I haven't even met and to you, Esther, well . . .

See you later, alligator (as one of my friends says).
Nicolas

John to Esther

Paris–Brussels, 22nd February 2019

Hello Esther,

I'm on a train for once. As you seem to be particularly interested in the weather, you should know that it's raining here. The gloomy countryside under the leaden grey sky is depressing me.

I reread the first letter I sent you. I come across as some miserable, despondent whinger. If I were you, I'd fire the tiresome blighter on the spot.

I was born and raised in Paris. My parents had four children—I was the second born. We were all sent to boarding school. After graduating from a prestigious military academy, my father forged a successful career for himself in the private sector, while my mother studied business. No one knows why, she probably doesn't either, and it doesn't actually matter. But once she was married she decided she wouldn't work. They married in church. My mother became deeply religious, but my father wasn't particularly devout. We lived on Avenue Foch. Our parents were strict; real sticklers for good manners and keeping up with the Joneses, but they were good sorts. However, they had one thing in common: they weren't cut out to have children. But what the Lord asks, the Lord gets . . . Unlike my father, my mother came from a very modest background. My maternal grandmother, Manine, whom I mentioned in my previous letter, worked as a sales assistant in a small department store in the seventeenth district of Paris. I think it's now been taken over by a chain. I felt right at home in that place. It was tiny compared to the huge stores like Galeries Lafayette and Printemps on the Boulevard Haussmann in the centre of Paris, where my mother used to drag me to kit me out for school. Manine darned stockings and tights for a living; a profession that practically disappeared along with her. The very last darner worked on Rue Tronchet, I'm told. Writing that, I get the impression that I was born in the nineteenth century. In short, she was friendly, funny, and outspoken. I was the favourite of all her grandchildren, and she didn't hide it. She had a rocky relationship with her only daughter. I guess it was since her daughter got married. "It's too much for me to think of my daughter as bigoted and rich, you understand, my darling," she confided to me. What saddened her the most was not so much that her daughter was now part of the bourgeoisie, but that she was ashamed of her mother's profession, to the point of asking her to give it up. She offered to support her if she didn't work. For Manine, this was out of the question. What my mother couldn't understand was how much my grandmother loved going to work in the morning. Manine was talented at meticulous work like this, which required skill and concentration. She was at ease with the customers who entrusted her with their stockings and tights, most of whom came from modest backgrounds like herself. She darned the nylon, concealed the scrapes, camouflaged the snags, and stopped the ladders. "I earn my keep", she would tell me proudly.

My parents willingly let me sleep over at her house on Saturday nights on one condition: that my grandmother accompany me to church the next morning, near her home in Levallois. She promised, but we only went once, just to learn the name of the priest and find the place. Manine was afraid that my mother would turn up without warning, so we spent the whole duration of the service in the bistro just opposite the church. I would sip a grenadine juice and she would order a beer, and we would play rummy while keeping an eye on the comings and goings outside. We had a plan: if one of us saw my mother, we would leave the café at top speed and slip into the church through the small side door which remained open during the service. My mother never came, however. I often wondered if we would have pulled off our plan. Looking back, I'm sure that my mother was aware of our tricks.

I used to visit my grandmother at the department store where she worked whenever I could. I loved watching her work, sat behind her little wooden table with the lamp, engrossed in her darning. I used to pass my time in the bookshop while waiting for her to finish up. I could spend hours exploring the different collections of children's books. Whenever a new Famous Five or Secret Seven came out, she would give it to me. They were more precious to me than the ones my parents bought me, or the ones I bought with my pocket money. Then we would take the bus back home to Levallois-Perret. Her fried potatoes were heaven on earth as was her courgette gratin with béchamel sauce. She spoilt me, and took me for picnics in the Boulogne woods where there was a children's amusement park. Sometimes we even went to the cinema on the Champs-Elysées. We had such fun. I loved my grandmother. She showered me with attention. I gave her the best of myself in return.

She came to ours every Christmas Eve, as did my paternal grandparents. They were very nice to us, but a bit standoffish. Or maybe it was me who was standoffish with them. I only saw them twice a year and didn't know them particularly well. Christmas Eve was always an ordeal. At home, in our vast Parisian flat, I didn't recognize Manine. She avoided my gaze. She looked like a tiny mouse, peeping out of the deep black leather armchair she had sunk into. She looked incongruous and out of place in the cold, designer décor. She didn't utter a word as she clutched her Baccarat champagne flute, petrified of dropping it. She didn't like champagne, and would have preferred a good beer, but that wasn't likely to happen. I could see how uncomfortable she looked. All I could do was smile at her, which she didn't see or pretended not to see. Our living room was three times the size of her studio flat. She was intimidated by our luxurious dwelling. I wanted to grab her hand so the pair of us could run back to hers and eat her delicious fried potatoes while slumped on her old, battered sofa in front of the telly. True partners in crime. We never talked about those awful Christmases and once it was over, we acted like it had never happened. It was easy to see why the mother daughter relationship was so difficult. To impress her mother, her daughter would put on a sumptuous spread, displaying her wealth in all its splendour. Whereas she should have sacrificed the pomp and ceremony and simply shown her mother humility, respect and affection.

Living in luxury reassured my mother. I wonder how she squared this guilty pleasure with her arrival at the Pearly Gates later on. It was a mystery. But she was unable to imagine that anyone could think differently to her. As for my grandmother, she made no effort to get closer to her daughter. She systematically criticized and rejected everything she said or did. I couldn't imagine them as a young mother and daughter under the same roof. Manine thought her son-in-law was morose. I think she felt sorry for him.

So that was my childhood. Some of it good, some of it bad. I didn't hate or love boarding school; I just went along with it. It was a nice place, most of the teachers were friendly and there was a good atmosphere. I made some very good friends there.

What about you, Esther? Tell me about yourself. All I know is that you live in Lille, you're a bookseller and you organize writing workshops. I would love to hear more.

Best wishes,
John

P.S. By the way, I thought we were supposed to state in our first letter what battles we're fighting. Does being our teacher make you exempt?

Esther to John

Lille, 28th February 2019

John,

I think that if he hadn't lost my mother to a stroke, my father would not have been so worried about me and so watchful of my every move. This was the man who had been a free spirit in his youth and spent his younger years backpacking around the world. But that was before. François Urbain never lived that way again.

If you like detective stories, François Perceval may ring a bell. It was his pen name. He was a secondary school French teacher until he retired from the education system at forty-three years old to devote himself to writing. He

would release a novel every two years, with the precision
of a Swiss watch, netting good sales. He wrote dark, bleak
crime fiction. He liked to keep his distance from his readers.
When he had to meet them at book fairs or bookshops, he
was hardly friendly. He was terse and gave them one-word
answers, hoping to get it over with as quickly as possible.
He barely smiled when they told him how much they enjoyed his novels. Despite this, I know he was flattered by
their compliments and recognition.

I appeared in all his novels; I was by turns the hero-
ine or a minor secondary character. I was a waitress in a
gloomy hotel bar in Paris, a museum attendant in Amster-
dam, a corpse fished out of the Loire River in Nantes, and
a missing woman in Arcueil. Physically, he portrayed me
as I really was, but mentally, he inflated my most prom-
inent character traits. At least, as he saw them. I could be
anything from funny to smart, stubborn to sulky or head
in the clouds. I grew up with his novels from the time I
could walk. I hated playing his corpses or victims. When
I complained to him, he would act surprised. "Why do
you think it's you? You haven't forgotten what a novel is,
have you?" he would reply, not waiting for my reaction.
His first source of inspiration for his writing was his melancholy. I was the second. Or maybe it was the other way
around.

I could feel his gaze on me when we went to the park
and I ran off to play. I could sense his concern when he
dropped me off at a birthday party. When I went on school
field trips I would see him waving madly outside the window of the school bus. If ever I had a mere headache, a
mole that looked suspicious, or a bout of indigestion, he
would whisk me off to the doctor. It was on 15th October 1982 in the late afternoon that my parents' world was
turned upside down. My father was sitting on the living

room sofa reading. My mother, Hélène, bent down to kiss him quickly before going out to buy apples. She was already running down the stairs of the building by the time he looked up from his book, *On Earth as it is in Heaven* by René Belletto. On her way home, my mother was just a few steps away from our building when she collapsed on the pavement. Her apples spilled out of the bag and rolled into the gutter. Her long, red hair messily hid her face, which had hit the concrete. She didn't move, as if she were asleep. Her brain was drowning in a pool of blood: a haemorrhage from a ruptured artery. The blood was gushing out with the force of a burst dam, destroying everything in its path. When the neighbour rang the doorbell to tell my father that Hélène had "collapsed", my father was turning the last page of his book. All that was left was the epilogue which reads as follows:

We were happy. I fed off her scent, her hair whose red lowlights were intensified by the glow of a lamp some distance from the bed, her young flesh, her slim, firm, elegant hands, which I clasped and kissed a thousand times, those same hands that stroked my body a thousand times.

Her coma was short lived. She didn't leave my father and the doctors any time to think about operating or worry about a second stroke, or the aftermath and possible after-effects, physiotherapy or special arrangements to be made . . . My mother gave them no time to dither or to hope. She was determined. She never could stand delays, prevarication and procrastination. With her, it was all or nothing. And she proved this one last time, by dying suddenly and unexpectedly.

Around six in the evening, my father was wondering whether the apple pie would be ready for dinner. The next morning at dawn, he was standing in a lift heading up to the morgue, his wife's body lying on a gurney, draped in a white sheet. He stood by her side and held her trailing hand tightly in his.

She was pronounced dead on 16th October 1982 at 3:03 am at the University Hospital in Lille. My father spent many minutes with his face buried in her hair "to capture her smell", he later wrote to me. "That mixture of geraniums and earth after the rain" as he put it. From that day on, he couldn't bring himself to eat apples, as if they were to blame. At the very sight of apple sauce or pie, he would turn his head away. He also ditched Rene Belletto's novel, never reading the closing lines. He'll never know how David Aurphet's whirlwind story ends. But I do. David Aurphet reminds me of my father. He was rather depressed, extremely cynical and had a gift for black humour.

I have no memories of my mother's death, of course. But my father has told me about it so many times that it has become an integral part of my life. I absorbed it like a sponge and turned it into my own personal reality. A few days after the funeral, he conducted his own investigation. He asked the greengrocer if he had noticed anything unusual about his wife's speech, her eyesight or her balance. The answer was no. He rummaged through his wife's drawers, found five-month-old blood test results and showed them to his doctor, hoping to spot an abnormally high level of white blood cells, platelets and lipids that had gone unnoticed or that my mother had deliberately concealed. But her results were impeccable. Hélène Urbain, a thirty-four-year-old sculptor, who never smoked, only drank on special occasions, ran every Sunday morning, and took tango lessons with her husband on Tuesdays, had had a long life ahead of her. My father was hoping to spot early tell-tale signs of his wife's death. He sought to shoulder the responsibility for it. It would have gladly given him an excuse to sink into despair.

I must have been seventeen years old when he finally eased his grip on me. It's absurd, when you think about it. That's the age at which your friends have just got their driving license, you drink too much, get offered drugs, and fall in love with the first idiot who comes along . . .

My father committed suicide three years ago, at home, without so much as a farewell note or an explanation. I've been in a rage ever since.

Though I describe him as an anxious, cold man, that's only partly true. He had a vivid imagination and was passionate. He passed his love of travel and literature on to me. During the holidays, we used to visit writers' houses. George Sand in Nohant-Vic, Balzac and Victor Hugo in Paris, Cervantes in Valladolid, in Spain, Colette in Saint-Sauveur-en-Puisaye, Jean de La Fontaine in Château-Thierry, and Edmond Rostand in the Basque Country. We even went to the States, visiting Steinbeck in Salinas, and Faulkner in Oxford. He gave me a wonderful childhood and adolescence.

Our childhood determines our adult lives. We all have different experiences which are more or less stable or reliable and which ultimately dictate our future fears, our weaknesses, our enthusiasm and our drive. Before going any further in our exchanges, I wanted to tell you about my past and it was important that you tell me about yours. Now it's done.

As the initiator of this project, I was going to skip the question that you have quite rightly asked me: "What battles are you fighting?" From what I just told you, I can say that first and foremost I'm battling anger.

Tell me why you think you betrayed your grandmother.

You are wrong about the weather. I don't care about it at all. I am surrounded by people who talk about it all day long, and want to know what the weather will be like in two hours, tomorrow, in a week's time . . . It's useful as it can help us know what to wear and get organized, depending on whether it's going to be dry or rainy, but this weather craze exasperates me. Or should I say it makes me nervous. I like waking up and discovering the weather when I open the curtains. A day of changeable weather is a day of surprises, which is good. I don't care if it's sunny or cold. I don't care if I look like an idiot in my dress and sandals when it's pouring, or in my boots and socks when it's hot as hell—not a common occurrence, I'll admit, when you live in Lille.

Best,
Esther

Every other year, I usually forget my cousin's birthday. This year, I didn't. I was even the first one to call him. It was Alma who picked up. Raphael was still sleeping. We talked for a while, before she put him on. I began the conversation by complaining. Why didn't he settle down with Alma? Why didn't they have children? She would end up leaving him and quite rightly so. After that, he would become a bitter, lonely old man. "I just love the way you wish me happy birthday early in the morning, dear cousin. It's a real treat," he said. We laughed and I asked him to forgive me. He told me how he planned to take Alma to Stockholm in June. And about a restaurant he would take us to the next time I was in Paris. He asked how it was going with my students. I imagine he was secretly smirking on the other end of the line, poking fun at my workshop. I didn't hide my enthusiasm from him. "I didn't expect it to be like this! They are using my workshop as a smokescreen to confide in each other and seek answers to existential questions that they cannot solve on their own. It's exciting and a bit confusing, but

I'm hanging on in there. You'd be shocked at how quickly they've opened up to each other. I think asking them the question 'What battles are you fighting?' at the first meeting and making them answer out loud, broke the ice. By the way, I wonder how you would have answered it?" Raphael just chuckled. "I struggle with not intruding on their privacy when we speak on the phone," I added. "I'm not their therapist, I'm their teacher." He was supportive and replied that he was sure I was doing a great job, because I knew how to temper my rigour with kindness. "Maybe you're right not wanting kids," I concluded. "The more I learn about them, the more I realize that parenting is a minefield; its challenges can push us over the edge and into the hands of evil forces. It's crazy what baggage we're all carting around with us."

Nicolas to Juliette

Paris, 25th February 2019

Juliette,

Maybe you came home too soon last time. We weren't ready for each other. I couldn't think straight; I needed time and space to get my head around what was happening to you and to us. I hope you don't take this the wrong way, but I'm glad we're having some time apart now. I never expected myself to say this. It's like surviving a tornado—you're in shock but alive. We spent months fighting and resenting each other. When you were pregnant, I didn't understand why you were so hard on yourself. It wasn't like you. I just thought you were tired and that everything would fall into place afterwards. We've talked about it enough, it's probably pointless to go over it again here on paper. We can't put the clock back, but it's become an obsession. Why did I not take the time to really think about things? How could I be satisfied with "it'll be better when the baby comes"? How could I have lived with you for sixteen years and not know you? How could you hide such important and vital things from me? You didn't trust me and I don't know why. I was furious; first with myself, then with you. When I said in the workshop that I was battling with guilt, you raised your beautiful eyebrows. The same eyebrows I used to love to kiss when I felt you needed it. You bit your lower lip; your way of saying that you weren't sure whether to believe me or not. Of course I feel remorse! When you were pregnant, I pretended everything was fine. Then, when Adele was born, I wasn't patient enough with you and refused to see how serious your condition was.

I don't know if you want to bring these things up again. I think we should. What do you think? We don't have much of a choice. All we can do is write to each other. If you want us to talk about Adele, it has to come from you.

When you go to pick her up, my mother is pleased to see you. Things are going very well between her and the little one, though I don't know why I'm telling you, as I'm sure you've seen that for yourself. I'm the one who's finding it hard. It's not much fun living with my mother again at forty-one years old. We're both making an effort. She has to return to Bourg-en-Bresse next weekend. My sister has offered to come and help me out, and I've accepted.

Please reply and tell me how you are doing. We've come this far, don't give up now.

N.

P.S. It would be helpful if you could collect your post.

Juliette to Nicolas

Malakoff, 28th February 2019

Nicolas,

If you only knew how much I would love to be able to tell you that I'm getting better and that slowly but surely things are getting back on track. Alas, I'm not there yet. Whenever there seems to be an improvement and I emerge from the abyss, I fall right back into it the very next day. Fortunately, when I'm in the bakery, I can hold it together and blot it out. Since I've changed my medication, I'm sleeping better, and it no longer takes me two hours to wake up.

I've moved to Malakoff and I'm living in the room next to the bakery, the one I used to use for storage. I feel safe in this tiny space. Since I'm on the premises I'm the one who opens up shop. Émeline and Antoine start later. Getting up at dawn reminds me of our first years together in Paris.

You're asking yourself stuff you don't need to. How can you believe that I kept things from you? I didn't hide anything from you, I hid them from myself. What are these "things" anyway? What went wrong at the start? What is this thing, this beast lying dormant inside of me that decided to rear its ugly head when Adele was born? And what about motherhood? For centuries, we've been led to believe it's the most magical time of our lives, haven't we? Total fulfilment? Guaranteed happiness? A dream come true? For me, childbirth was my descent into hell. You have no idea how much it hurts. I don't want to go back to the root of all this. But my therapist is forcing me to. When Esther asked me what battles I was fighting, there were many things I could have said; my struggles with abandonment, insanity, wanting to die, running away, anger, or simply feeling like I was going under, submerged. I didn't hesitate. I chose the last one. In the early months of my depression I was drowning, engulfed by life, and it was the most terrifying sensation I have ever experienced.

When I pick up Adele, I make the time to talk to your mother. I'm not comfortable with it though. She knows me well enough to notice. She moved into our home to take care of our daughter because of me. And she's doing a great job. I can't find the words to express my gratitude to her. And yet I can't help but hate her at the same time. She has taken my place beside Adele. Yet I left a vacancy for her. I'm aware of that. I'm embarrassed; my head's all over the place. I'm just one big contradiction, aren't I? Isn't that what you're thinking right now? You're right. I am hateful, infuriating and a mess. A complete waste of space.

I trust you; but I don't trust myself. You have nothing to blame yourself for. You did what you could. No one could have foreseen what would happen to me.

Why won't you talk to me about Adele; why does it have to come from me?

With much love and affection,
Juliette

Absence

Jean to Juliette

Verjus-sur-Saône, 27th February 2019

Dear Juliette,

I knew virtually nothing about postpartum depression before reading your letter. I wouldn't have known the difference between that and the baby blues. As the wife of a medical doctor this is rather embarrassing!

I loved being pregnant. For someone who didn't want a child, motherhood was a real eye-opener for me. Aurélie was a very lively and headstrong child. Her father was totally devoted to her. I lost count of the number of hikes they went on together, and the number of slopes they skied down. Up to the age of fifteen, Aurélie was not a particularly bright student. She barely scraped through to the next class up each year. Her father and I didn't put any pressure on her. I didn't manage to pass on my love of music to her, unfortunately.

She excelled at sports, especially basketball and athletics. One evening, when she was sixteen, she announced quite seriously that she wanted to become a doctor. Naturally her father was delighted, but we both thought it was just a phase she was going through. Like idiots, we even sniggered about it. She proved us wrong, however, and went to medical school in Paris before becoming a gynaecologist. She was twenty-one years old when her father died. She first practised in a hospital in Paris, then decided to do humanitarian work. She wanted to travel and help the less fortunate. She was a child with ants in her pants, who wouldn't sit still, so travelling halfway round the world whenever she could reflected her personality. She worked in many parts of Africa, eventually settling in the Central African Republic. Though we had been awfully close to start with, slowly but surely she started to distance herself from me. At first, she would come back for three weeks in the summer. Then two. Then it dwindled to nothing. The first three years she didn't come back, I offered several times to go out there and join her. She always had a good excuse to put me off. She either didn't know where she was going to be on those dates, or the area was too dangerous, or it was precisely the moment she was planning to return to France, etc. etc. I couldn't accept being cut out of her life so I persevered. Then sometime later she sent me a brief message cancelling again. I called her, wrote to her, sent email after email. Her answers could not have been briefer: "Hello Mum. Thanks for your message. Don't worry about me. I'm doing fine. I hope you are too. Lots of love." I've dug out some of her other old letters, Juliette. Here's one of them: "I can't have you to stay right now. Maybe later on, but we'll talk about it when the time comes. Lots of love."

I don't know when and where I went wrong. I must have missed or misinterpreted something. I should have just gone over there, just the once, without telling her. I shouldn't have given her the choice. That way I would have seen what I didn't want to see or couldn't see. I wasn't brave enough, however. I didn't dare turn up uninvited. I went over my memories of the two of us at least a hundred times and couldn't find anything. What happened to us, where did we go wrong? Has she done something objectionable, or unforgiveable? I nearly went insane raking over the past, searching for clues to help me fathom out the answer. My brain was frazzled, alas all for nothing as I hit a dead end each time.

After one of her emails, in which she coldly wished me a merry Christmas, with no affection or concern for me at all, I decided that enough was enough and that I wouldn't write to her any more. She obviously didn't think I was worth the effort. I was no longer going to beg. I sadly deduced that I was trying to make her pity me. I was sick of forcing myself on her and trying to understand why she was like this. I had shown her enough times how concerned I was. Besides, she didn't hesitate to let me know she was sick of my questions. After years of battling with her, I was a nervous exhausted wreck. I hoped my silence would make her react, but it didn't. I was going to have to live with it. This emptiness in my stomach, this vast unreplaceable void . . . There's not a day goes by that I don't think about her. Every year she sends me an email for my birthday, and one for Christmas. I reply with the same casual tone. She doesn't even seem surprised at this. She no longer tells me that she'll be back next summer. My new attitude must have removed a millstone from around her neck. I've achieved that, if nothing else.

We don't have to accept bad behaviour from our children and forgive everything they do. The pain hasn't gone away, I've just learnt to live with it. And I'm doing better than I was.

Jean

Juliette to Jean

Malakoff, 5th March 2019

Good evening Jean,

I don't think I told you that in my bakery on Rue de Montreuil I have a wood-fired oven. It is one of the latest. In this line of business, staff turnover is high. I used to get too attached to my employees. I would fantasize that we were one big family, learning from each other, growing together, as a team, but above all as friends. Some were talented bakers, but all of them ended up deserting me. The work was too hard, too poorly paid. They didn't like the early starts or the late and unsocial hours, often working on weekends. I was furious each time one of them left. Why on earth did they go into baking then? When I quit my BA to go into breadmaking, I knew what to expect. But they looked blindsided by it all. Whoops, they got it wrong, they didn't imagine it would be this tough. Some wanted to travel and not feel tied down or give in to routine. Others went to work for chains which churned out bread on an industrial scale. The money was better and the hours were more regular. I couldn't refrain myself from giving them a piece of my mind: "So that's it then, you prefer to make bread that tastes like crap and live like a couch potato? Well go on then! You've got a great future ahead of you." The truth is that I was furious that I couldn't afford to pay them more. When I opened my first bakery, the bank was keeping a close eye on my finances. And, swept along in the daily rush, I forgot all good intentions to encourage and praise them more. I was finally forced to admit that you can enjoy baking without throwing your heart and soul into it. Not everyone is as focused or ambitious about it as me. I had to learn to be more understanding and less obsessive. This is another reason I love my job: it has changed me for the better. I lacked tolerance and compassion. I was like a lump of dough fresh out of the fridge, too hard and too cold. I needed warming up, kneading and massaging to make me smoother and more pliable.

Best regards,
Juliette

Jean is both annoyed and disconcerted. Did Juliette get her last letter? There's not a word about Aurélie. She would have appreciated a little sympathy. It wasn't easy pouring her heart out about her daughter's absence. Another astonishing thing is that Juliette doesn't even mention her depression. What a peculiar way to behave, suddenly switching to talking about opening her bakery and her recruitment problems.

Jean rereads Juliette's previous letter, dated 24th February. This was when she first mentioned her postpartum depression, though she couldn't yet talk about her own case, for fear of relapsing. Maybe this is just a small diversion until she feels ready. Jean decides to let Juliette take the lead and let her make the first move.

Nicolas to Juliette

Paris, 3rd March 2019

Juliette,

As soon as I walk through the front door, your absence hits me. It leaps right into my face and knocks me to the ground. I get up and act as if nothing has happened. My mother and Adele are there waiting for me.

I like the fact you're contradictory. You say it like it's new. You've always been that way. But not as bad, I agree. Anyway, we're not writing to each other to spare each other's feelings but to move forward. If we're not sincere with each other and avoid confrontation we'll just hit a brick wall. You've been rejecting me for months, staring at me blankly as if I were a stranger. Or, even worse, as if I was your enemy, when you couldn't look after Adele and I had to do it for you. I want you to be harsh and angry with me.

I want to hear some emotion. Anything is better than indifference or loathing. You're doing better. You're working again and spending two half-days a week with Adele at the maternity unit. You're making progress with your therapist. I only wish I had been more patient. I hate myself for not realizing what was happening to you. During all those years we spent together I should have asked you more about your childhood. I thought that you had somehow come to terms with it. I can see how naive I was. I shouldn't have accepted your silence on the subject. It was too easy for me, and lazy of me too.

Yes, if you want us to talk about Adele, I do believe the initiative has to come from you. Can you do it without feeling more sadness, guilt, or whatever? I must be sure. In your letters you don't write that you want to talk about her. You simply ask me why I don't. Anyway, if you can, and if you want to, tell me how it's going with her at the maternity unit.

Everything is fine at the restaurant, despite the staffing problems. Yannick is off sick (chicken pox, at thirty-five!), so is Bernadette (bronchitis), so it's been manic all week. As soon as they get back, I'll start working on "blandness". I owe this urge to Philippe, who came to lunch last week and gave me François Jullien's book *Éloge de la fadeur*, a tribute to blandness. I knew that in Chinese culture, unlike in the west, blandness doesn't have negative connotations. Although I didn't know that it was a flavour in its own right! I discovered its origins, the schools that inspired it, the philosophy behind it, and that it's considered a form of artistic ideal. It sits on the fence, refusing to be categorized. Not sweet, not mild, not sour/acidic. François Jullien writes that it leaves room for "savouring" and experimentation. In Chinese and Japanese cuisine, bland is associated with the purity of water, and the quest for serenity. It's fascinating.

I must ditch my obsession with citrus fruits. After lunch, Philippe waited for me and drove me home. He wanted to see Adele. He says she's looking more and more like you, except for the eyes. He asked after you. He says hi. He wanted me to tell him why you left us again, but I dodged his question. For some weird reason I can't talk about it with my mates. I'm afraid I'll say something stupid or embarrassing, so I prefer to keep my mouth shut. It's hard to talk about this damn illness.

Take care of yourself.
N.

From the window, Nicolas can see a young woman on the pavement opposite pulling up the metal shutter of her bakery. The sky is blue without a cloud in sight. It's a splendid Parisian Sunday morning. It's early still. He tiptoes to his daughter's room, taking care not to make a sound. He knows how easily she wakes. The light streams in through the window catching the fabric bunnies on her mobile. He leans gently over her crib. Adele is awake. She's looking at the ceiling. Her fixed gaze and her silence alarm him. His heart starts pounding. How long has she been awake? He smiles at her, puts his hand in her baby grow, and sniffs her bottom; good, her nappy doesn't need changing. He wonders if she is okay, and whether she is suffering from her mother's absence. She is healthy, is gaining weight and has a good appetite, but can she pick up on her mother's distress? Will this have any long-term effects on her? He takes her in his arms and hugs her. "But why don't you call for me if you can't sleep, my precious one? We're a bit lost without mummy, but we're not doing so badly, are we? Oh my darling! I'm so sorry for all this. Your mummy loves you, she'll be back soon. It's not your fault, angel.

Yes, she will be back. When she's better, you'll see what a tough cookie she is. A chatterbox that can't shut up, with a hundred ideas buzzing around in her head at once. Believe me, after a day with her, you'll sleep like a log. But we must be patient. I know you miss her and I know that it's hard for a baby to be separated from her mother; it's not fair and it's a waste. But I'm here. I should have told you all this before; sorry my beauty, sorry my sweetheart, my darling." Nicolas holds her tightly against him. And for the first time, he starts to cry; tears run down his cheeks and onto his daughter's neck. His words come out jumbled but each sentence he utters is a release. He stretches out his arms and holds his daughter up in the air and looks at her. Adele smiles at him.

Juliette to Nicolas

Malakoff, 13th March 2019

Nicolas,

What I suffered in the months following Adele's birth was indescribable. I couldn't talk about it, even to you. I didn't know how to put my meltdown into words. I could have said something like: "I don't feel anything for my baby." Then, a few weeks later, I could have said, "I'm petrified of my baby, I can't cope, it's all too much for me. She needs protecting, not me." Such words are despicable, I know. But what would you have done then, Nicolas? No one could understand what I was going through. I was totally on my own and a danger to my baby. I remember you sitting next to me and I was delirious. I remember the doctor announcing that my baby blues had turned into postpartum depression, and I felt a strange kind of relief.

I couldn't think straight, my main concern was to stop the anxiety attacks before they spiralled out of control (I completely failed on that front), but at that very second I realized that if what I was suffering from had a name, then others were suffering from it too.

You wrote that I should have told you more about my childhood. You blame yourself for not broaching the subject. If you had, I would have told you I was fine. I would have said that being given up for adoption hadn't traumatized me. I didn't perceive any after-effects. Those first chaotic days of my life were eclipsed by my wonderfully happy childhood. Nineteen years of bliss with my adoptive parents, who pampered, loved and cherished me, never hiding the truth about my birth from me. A child couldn't wish for a better relationship with their parents. My one regret was that my birth mother didn't leave me a note explaining why she did it, or something to remind me of her, as she was most certainly encouraged to do. You know all this anyway. I wasn't dodging the subject, as you seem to think. I answered your questions at the time. I wasn't lying or twisting the truth when I said that being abandoned at birth hadn't traumatized me. When Adele was born it resurfaced, however, like a dormant volcano erupting and destroying everything in its path, turning it all to ashes. That was the bit I wasn't expecting.

I behaved badly towards my parents. By refusing to see them, and depriving them of their granddaughter, I was punishing them. The best parents in the world. When I'm ready I'll call them, or rather I'll send them a letter. I would never have thought of writing a letter to them before the workshop, but it's a great solution. That way they won't hear me crying, stammering, gasping for breath as I ask for their forgiveness, and tell them how much I love them.

I have since discovered that not knowing one's birth parents and being abandoned causes great suffering. Although I can talk and write about it now, I still have to accept it. This is what I'm working on with my psychiatrist. My suffering doesn't take anything away from the marvellous childhood Anne and Maxime gave me.

The doctors at the maternity unit tell me I'm getting better, and that contact between Adele and me is getting easier and more natural. I have a hard time convincing myself of this. I still have panic attacks if I am left alone with her for too long. They assure me that they are more spaced out than before. All it takes is for Adele to be a little grumpy, or half asleep, or for me to misinterpret what she wants and it triggers them. I'm convinced that I am incapable of looking after her, that it's all my fault and I start to cry. When I talk to her, I avoid catching her eye (and she avoids mine too!), so I force myself to look at her, as they have advised me to do. We are currently learning to play together. She loves blocks. For the past two weeks she has been learning to stand up, so I help her hold on, and move from one place to another. The session ends with a discussion with the psychiatrist and the nurses. Then it's time to leave. I wonder when she will start crawling. Yes, I would like you to tell me about Adele, or rather about you and her. It will help me to get to know her better, and to take the initiative when I'm with her. You ask me not to be sad when you tell me about the good times you spend with her. How can I? Try to understand, Nicolas. I haven't been in her life all this time! You, on the other hand, you see her every day, you look after her, feed her, play with her, rock her, take her for walks, know what she likes, what makes her laugh and cry. While I only spend two half-days a week with her, surrounded by specialists who analyze our every move. I'm jealous, but this is nothing compared to the jealousy I felt before I was hospitalized. It was totally directed against Adele at that time. You were happy with your daughter and unhappy with me. You did everything better than me. I was the worst mother in the world. The hardest bit was in the evenings, when it was quiet outside and Adele couldn't fall asleep and would start crying. Her cries would echo through the flat, getting louder and louder. I couldn't get them out of my head, and the noise was driving me mad. "I can't do it, I don't understand what you want, Adele." Those endless hours alone with her. When were you going to come back from the restaurant? I ended up screaming at her: "Just sleep! I can't take it any more!" Then you would return, tired out but oh so calm. You would take her in your arms, rock her, soothe her. Everything got better. I hated the smiles, and the cuddles you lavished on her. I felt useless. This child was taking up all the space, slowly destroying me. She didn't love me. I kept thinking that if I hadn't had her, I wouldn't have gone crazy.

Please don't get angry, don't judge me. This is what was going through my mind; I can finally talk about it now.

I envy the bond you have with her, which is getting stronger every day. I'll never get back those lost moments; they're gone forever.

With much love and affection,
Juliette

John to Esther

Paris–Chicago, 3rd March 2019

Dear Esther,

My plane is currently experiencing severe turbulence, hence my scrawl. We left late because of a storm over Paris. It actually ending up hitting us over the Atlantic.

You ask me why I think I betrayed my grandmother. Because it wasn't long before I discovered the joys of money and behaved like a fool. Do you think that my grandmother, a darner by trade, who did her accounts every month in her notebook, and who was proud of her savings book to see her through the "hard times", who went without to pay for my weekend trips, would have appreciated seeing me squander money like this? I was taking my finals when she died of a heart attack.

When I had to make my first lay-offs, I had a guilty conscience, but it didn't last. My remorse was insignificant compared to my salary. Money is our primary motivation, we're happy as hell to get our hands on it. But once we become rich, it's difficult, if not impossible, to march in time with the rest of the world, to maintain a sense of proportion and know the value of money. We write expense reports without question, we can buy almost anything we want, we hand over our credit cards without even glancing at the amount, products don't attract us if their price tag isn't high enough. If we feel guilty, we write a big fat check to charity. I do this. Money is my backbone, it's there all the time, when I eat, negotiate, breathe, buy, sell, make love, feel guilty, or don't feel guilty. Without it, I don't know how to enjoy myself, how to love, or how to get up in the morning. Money can do anything and everything. It has me wrapped around its little finger. It controls every single cell in my body and makes my heart race. I hate it. I love it. Without it, who am I? What am I? I wish I knew.

This'll shock you, but I see suicide as a courageous act, and one I respect. To choose the day you're going to die is the ultimate freedom. Notwithstanding that it is extremely violent for the loved ones left behind. Some even deem it a cowardly way to solve your problems. I hope you have no regrets or remorse towards your father. You shouldn't.

We can do a lot for the people we love, but we can't do everything.

To wrap up, I have two unconnected questions for you. First, why didn't your father (his name doesn't ring a bell, but I'm not a fan of thrillers) remarry after your mother died? Second, as a bookseller, what gave you the idea for the writing workshop?

Best,
John

Esther to John

Lille, 9th March 2019

Hello John,

As I mentioned in my last letter, my father and I lived in Lille, just twenty minutes from each other. Yet we still sent each other letters. "Real letters?" people ask me when I talk about our special bond. Yes, *real letters*. Written on nice paper with a pen, put in an envelope with a stamp and left in the good care of the post office. Like we're doing now. We became pen pals a few months after I flew the nest. I was twenty years old and reluctant to leave him on his own, so he kindly gave me a push. I had to find a job as a student. He would help me pay the rent, but he thought I should stand on my own two feet. I didn't dare ask him right away how that first evening went without me. I was afraid he would just smirk and say, "It went very well. Why are you asking anyway? Come on, you don't live that far away!" Much later on, in one of my letters, I took the plunge and asked him. He gave a three-word answer: "It was terrible."

Being pen pals didn't stop us from meeting up and having wonderful conversations face to face too. I do miss his letters . . . Once a week we would meet early in the morning at the local café. I would sit next to him. We loved people-watching and commenting on their clothes, looks, quirks, etc. We were delighted if exotic-seeming blended families sat near us, though you don't see many in Lille's bistros at that time in the morning. We loved guessing who was who and how they were related. Sometimes we were even lucky enough to witness a domestic dispute. Our ears would prick up at the juicy details but we would carry on talking, resisting the urge to stare. This technique worked every time. When we parted, we would make a brief reference to our correspondence: "I wrote to you," "You'll get my letter," "Oh, by the way, I wrote back." Right from the start, we set the ground rules by making a distinction between the spoken word and the written word. The first should not tarnish or compromise the second. My daughter, Pia, thought that my father and I were "weird", and that talking by Skype or phone was easier. I extolled the virtues of our special letter writing relationship to her on several occasions, but to no avail.

Our letters could be a few lines or several pages long. We managed to write to each other fairly regularly. We complemented each other well; sometimes I would be feeling lazy, while he would be motivated. And vice versa. We wrote about our respective childhoods, Lille and the surrounding region, which I was as attached to as he was, his admiration for his grandfather—a coal miner—, my mother's beauty (a recurrent theme), how they met (another recurrent theme), and her absence that he still hadn't come to terms with since losing her when I was just three. Her death gnawed away at him still. He even wrote to me that he had "stopped fighting it". There were other topics too: his books, his reading material, his girlfriends, my daughter, old age, his friends and mine, motherhood, fatherhood . . . This might lead one to assume that our morning conversations were laborious and pale in comparison. But that couldn't be further from the truth. If anything, our exchanges in person were lighter and funnier.

In the early years, all his letters ended with a postscript containing his corrections: "It was very funny hearing about your conversation with Pia's teacher, but you get too bogged down in the details. It's a pity . . ." or "Why do you use the word 'always' so much? I counted three of them", or even "What's with all these exclamation marks? Read your previous letter out loud to yourself and you'll see there's a punctuation problem; the reader has no idea when he's allowed to breathe." Over time, his postscripts dwindled, then disappeared altogether. This sadly didn't mean that my writing had become perfect. He had merely got tired of correcting me. Or felt that I was too old to be corrected. I really missed his helpful comments.

It was in memory of our letter writing that I had this urge, two years after his death, to create a letter writing workshop. I missed him and his letters. I foolishly checked my letterbox every day, even a year after his death, expecting and hoping to find a letter from him. I was mad at him for not being more like the writer Romain Gary, who, in *Promise at Dawn*, claimed to have received nearly two hundred and fifty letters from his mother while he was at the front during the Second World War. On his return home in 1944, he learned that she had died three and a half years earlier, just months after he left. Fiction or reality, smoke and mirrors, a wild goose chase, a double take . . . Think what you will but I find the story beautiful and romantic. My father and I enjoyed citing it. Since he was determined to die, he could have done the same for me. He knew what his suicide would do to me . . . Why didn't he offer me this one last pleasure and continue our correspondence from "up there"? Just one last letter? I was surprised he hadn't cooked up a morbid joke of this sort. His books are full of them.

"You can do a lot for the people you love, but you can't do everything." You're right. Thank you. Thanks to you, I don't feel so guilty. After my father's death, I reacted the same way he did after my mother's death. I rummaged through his papers, scrutinized his medical records, called his friends . . . There had to be a reason. Did he have some terminal illness and didn't tell me? Was he depressed and I hadn't noticed? My search was futile. All I found out was that he was anaemic, had rheumatism, and was due to have a knee operation in a year. Nothing serious. Well, except for this: for the first time ever, I couldn't find any manuscripts on his desk. I went through his drawers, his computer. Nothing. Not the slightest trace of a work in progress. He always started his new novel a few weeks after handing in the last. He had finished his latest book, *It'll Snow Tonight*, more than a year before. I'm sure his death had something to do with writing. I may not have realized how vital it was for him to write every day.

Death often came up in his letters. He didn't fear it. On the contrary, old age, which he described as "debasing and degrading", terrorized him. Fascinated and repulsed by the physical decaying of the human body, he needed to describe it in all its horror: "Drooling on the chin, trembling hands, legs that won't move, towel around the neck, incontinence pads, underpants and socks that are impossible to get on without help." This is just a taster. He could be even more cynical. He didn't spare me any of the trials of senile dementia, of "these frail old bodies who wander around not remembering anything, stripped of their past, and their memories, one day asking their own children 'who are you?'" He would exclaim in horror whenever he saw a report in the press or on TV about the infantilization of residents in state-run nursing homes; he was aghast at how effortlessly their dignity was stripped from them.

When he heard that one of his acquaintances or friends had Alzheimer's, he would give me all the sordid details to make sure I thought the same as he did, that life is a bitch. Naturally, he passed on his fear of growing old to me.

I must have been twenty-five when he started to mention suicide in his letters. "I have every intention of choosing the day I die. What scares me, however, is messing it up." I made him swear that if he was going to do it, he would tell me. A fool's promise. I knew he wouldn't, but it made me feel better.

There was nothing morbid in what he said. On the contrary, he liked to joke about it. He thought he would know exactly when to do it. "Esther," he wrote, "you mustn't blame me. I know how angry you can get. When I'm dead, I would like you to spare me your anger, it's unnecessary." He still talked about it occasionally, but I no longer took it seriously.

On that particular morning, I waited for him for an hour at the café where we were due to meet. His phone rang and rang. I went back home to get the keys to his flat. I was afraid that he had fallen or fainted. Not for a second did I consider he had taken his own life. I found him lying on his bed, in the foetal position wearing the pyjamas I had given him for his last birthday. On his bedside table, he had left this note: "As promised . . . My time has come." He was seventy-four years old.

What do you want to know about my bookshop? It's in the centre of Lille. I mainly sell fiction, but I have a large section devoted to travel: classic guidebooks, essays and memoirs—both historical and contemporary—, maps, atlases, and photography books. I often eat lunch in Dutilleul Square, just next door, with a book. I love this long narrow park with its neatly arranged trees, flowerbeds and lawns. I work hard but I'm lucky to have had a helping hand along the way. I didn't go into this line of work to make a fortune. Without my father's financial support, I wouldn't have lived quite as comfortably. After his death, I discovered that I wasn't the only one who had benefited from his generosity. He financed part of the cost of a nursing home in Lens for one of his best friends and helped a former girlfriend make ends meet. He left me some money. One day, I'll take that trip of a lifetime to Japan, and I'll carry on helping his two friends as long as I can. I should sell his flat on Rue Ratisbonne, but I don't have the courage to yet. We moved there after my mother died and it was my home until I was twenty.

My father didn't remarry. He had many relationships, some longer and more serious than others. The good, the bad and the downright ugly, as I thought of them. More often ugly than good, it must be said.

I don't know what to make of your relationship with money; it's so alien to me. I waver between two extremes: jealousy or pity. Why do you talk about it in the past tense?

Best wishes,
Esther

P.S. As I was writing to you, I received this news alert on my phone: "Threatened by the digital age, will writing by hand become extinct?" Is this workshop a good idea?

It hasn't stopped raining since this morning. The bookshop was deserted. I was a little bored and would gladly have

gone for a walk. It was about six o'clock, and I still had
an hour to go before meeting Sophie at a chic new hotel
bar which had just opened in Lille. A white Martini would
soon lift my sullen mood. The first subject I will broach
with my friend, who is headmistress of a private secondary
school in the city, will be her favourite topic: the advantages
and disadvantages of living in Paris, Lille and the country.
"What would you advise me to do?" she always asked. And
I'd reply, "Leave Lille, since you keep asking yourself that
question." But her feet were still stuck firmly in the starting
blocks, as she had never left.

My phone was ringing. I didn't recognize the number.
Not concentrating, I picked up. "Hello, Dr Montgermon
here, I hope this isn't a bad time." It wasn't a question so I
had no choice but to listen. The psychiatrist said she hoped
we would have the opportunity to meet once the workshop
was over. She wanted to hear how I came up with the idea
for the workshop and whether it was living up to my expectations. And then, how about working together again in
the future? Her methods, she confided in me, were not always to the liking of her colleagues, who deemed them too
original and eclectic. She felt that in her profession, new
experiences and curiosity were essential tools. There were
many ways to help patients, but it was important to find a
strategy that was tailored to the individual. We could discuss this later, she said. In fact, she was calling to thank me.
"Of course, it's early days, but one of Juliette's letters to
Jean was a significant step towards her recovery." I barely
had time to tell her that I had had little to do with Juliette's recovery. She went on to say that in this particular
letter, her patient had taken stock of her own situation. She
had described the illness in its broadest terms as well as its
most obvious symptoms. Above all, and most importantly,
Juliette Esthover had shown compassion and concern for all

women who suffer from postnatal depression. And therefore herself. I find Dr Montgermon rather irritating, but this time I'm glad she called.

Jean to Samuel

Verjus-sur-Saône, 6th March 2019

Hello Samuel,

I am very sorry to hear about your brother. You must have had an exceedingly difficult time. Don't be too hard on your mother. Just because she cries every night doesn't mean that they are crocodile tears. I don't know her, but I highly doubt it. She is a prison nurse, so she is clearly a responsible person. She looks after the prisoners, listens to them, gives them support. Once she's back home and on her own, it's understandable that she vents her grief. You have to deal with your own pain, but also with your parents' pain. It's hard to watch our parents suffering and to feel powerless in the face of their misfortune. It's a hell of a burden for one man to bear.

My husband died of a heart attack. We were on holiday in Tanzania. He was fifty-nine years old. He was the best thing that ever happened to me, my dream man. If I had gone first, I can imagine what he would have done. He would have ridden his bike for miles, stopped somewhere in the mountains and screamed until his vocal cords collapsed. I managed to keep it together until his body was repatriated and he was buried, and Aurélie left for Paris two days later to take her exams. Then I got into bed. I slept, day and night, until I lost track of time. I hardly ate, stopped washing, and turned off my phone. I wanted to die of a broken heart. At some point, your body refuses to obey. It won't let you sleep. All you can do is learn to live again without your loved one.

You write that it is impossible for you and your parents to talk about Julian together. I have given this some consideration. At times, I too have not been able to communicate with my nearest and dearest. It's an impossible situation to escape. How can we break the glass wall that separates us from others without being tactless, without being rejected, without making them suffer even more? We prefer to act like we haven't noticed anything and that everything is normal. As if we didn't see, didn't understand, didn't hear. This silence must be broken, however. It destroys us. It's poison.

I have a daughter, Aurélie. She is a doctor and lives in China with her husband. I don't see her often. As for my animals, I have cows, pigs, a horse and a donkey. They all have one thing in common: they are rescue animals that I took in. I treat them with kindness so that they can live out their last days in comfort.

I don't know you well enough to say if you are cut out for higher education or not. What I do know is that you are wrong about reading. It's an open door to the world, to human nature, to past and future centuries. It's impossible that no subject interests you, that no literary genre appeals to you. Reading opens doors for us. I can accept, however, that you don't have the key to the door. Are you afraid to go into a bookshop or a library? The people who work there are there to help you, not judge you. Esther can tell you more about that. So stand tall, puff out your chest, take a deep breath, and tell yourself that you're a good person who has the right to be curious about the world. You have nothing to lose and everything to gain.

Keep me posted.
Jean

Samuel to Jean

13th March

Hello Jean,

When Julian was alive, I always felt in the way in this family. Now it's kind of worse. I don't know what my parents see when they look at me and talk to me. Maybe it's all in my head. How am I supposed to act? Who am I without my brother? An only child? The prodigal son? The substitute son? Or should I continue to keep my head down? My parents are cool with me, that's not the problem. They both like to hug me. They try their hardest to act as if nothing has happened. But I don't think this is helping me. You could cut the atmosphere with a knife in our flat, and there's nothing any of us can do about it.

The last few weeks when Julian was in hospital, I was angry because his long absence wasn't a good sign. My brother's cancer had taken over. Yet all I could think about was moving into his room which was bigger than mine, as he wasn't there any more. I had had enough of his illness, which we all dragged around with us like a leaden weight. It stopped us from moving forward, from loving each other and yelling at each other like normal families do. Sometimes I wished he would die just to get it over with. I still felt sad, but yes, I did have such thoughts, I'm not going to lie. Since then I tell myself that if I had supported him more, and believed he would get better, if I hadn't wished him dead, he would still be alive today. Not cured, but alive. Now that he's gone, I'm ashamed that I wanted his room. How could I have been so horrible and uncaring? Me and my parents ended up partly clearing it out. I suspect they did this for my sake, otherwise they would have just left it, pretending he had just gone away for a while. They asked me if I wanted it cleared out completely. I wanted his bookshelves to remain as they were. And his desk too. This made my mum feel better. The rest we cleared out, packed into boxes and carried down into the basement. My mum refused to throw anything away. My dad brought the wine bottles upstairs to make space. This meant they didn't intend going back down there again. I know what it cost us to clear out his room. For me, it was worse than his funeral. All memories of him gone, packed into boxes and taped up. Within the space of a few hours, hardly a trace of him remained. What's a man's life worth? Nothing.

Julian always got good marks in French; he loved reading. In fact books were the only things he tidied away in his room; that made Mum laugh. That's why I didn't want anyone to touch his bookshelves or his desk. So instead of going to a bookshop to buy books, I decided that I would read them all, one by one, starting with the top shelf, from left to right. I want to put my eyes where he put his, on the same words, discover the same stories as him, the same characters. Afterwards, I'll put the books back exactly as I found them. I may not understand a word, who knows? Sometimes he'd say to me: "If you read, you wouldn't be so stupid." The first book is called *Reunion* by Fred Uhlman. Luckily, it's not too long. I'll try to start it tomorrow. Have you read it?

Don't you want to tell me more about your animals? You don't say much about your daughter.

You know it's crazy, but I can no longer bear the sound of masking tape being unrolled.

Speak to you soon,
Samuel

John to Nicolas

Paris–Tunis, 11th March 2019

Hello Nicolas,

Oh my! "The culinary poet", "The two-star nerd", is that
what they call you? The articles I read on you emphasize
your poetic side; your love of words being the inspiration behind some of your dishes. You asked me if I cook. A little. My
specialties are fried eggs, pasta in tomato sauce, and frozen
soups . . .

It can't be easy what you are going through, but you seem
like a courageous guy. The negative image you have of your
wife will eventually fade I suppose. My advice and encouragement stop here, you know why . . .

I hate to come across as some disillusioned depressive.
You're not the first to point this out to me so I'd better get
used to it. You're right to say that it's impossible to succeed
in our respective careers without putting serious energy
into our jobs every day. Lately, I've had to dig a little deep-
er to find mine, but I still manage. For how long though?
Making money was my driving force for so many years; not
any more.

I used to thrive on challenges. The greater the challenge, the more people messed with me, the better I got.
You asked why I don't delegate more. Right now, it's
tricky. One of my primary tasks involves reviewing con-
tracts with customer service departments abroad. It's a
rotten job. Basically, I fire poor people who are already
badly paid because they haven't met their targets and hire
others whom I pay even less. I'm also supposed to win
new international markets.

Nicolas, I trust you not to repeat any of this. I don't know
you, but I trust you. Reckless of me don't you think?

My flat does indeed overlook the Tuileries gardens. That's why I bought it. I'm on the fifth floor. It's noisy, but that doesn't bother me. I spend my time travelling, from city to city, so the days go by in a blur. I think I'm scared of a void taking hold and having to face myself. How do you cope with loneliness, knowing nobody is waiting for you? I'm not complaining. I have girlfriends from time to time, which suits me. I get to enjoy the good times, without the constraints of being tied down. I'm free . . . If I'd met the love of my life, I probably wouldn't be talking like this. I wish I were in love and that someone loved me back. I miss that wonderful feeling of sheer ecstasy and excitement you have every second of the day. The fireworks and the racing heart, anchoring you in the present, painting the future in a glorious new light. I wish I had all that . . . it's so remote. You must be shocked; the hard-faced businessman has a heart after all.

I forgot to tell you about my children. Next time, I promise.

John

P.S. By the way, I find your way of addressing Esther when you write to me rather irritating.

Nicolas to John

Paris, 18th March 2019

Hello John,

Sometimes I fantasize about closing my restaurant, taking my daughter and opening up a bistro out in the sticks, far away from all this shit. Bye Uhlmann stress, sky high rents, idiots on wheels, Michelin stars, activists trashing the city, police who crack trying to stop them, and the homeless whom I don't even notice any more. I can picture myself in a big house in the country with Adele, a dog, a blazing fire in the hearth and a nice peaceful life. Yesterday, I had a drink with a friend in a dingy bistro near the Eiffel Tower, where they had the gall to charge me fifty cents for the slice of lemon in my Perrier! I complained to the owner asking if it was a joke. Looking offended, he said did I think the lemons fell out of the sky? He had to pay for them, so why should he give them away free? I replied: "Because you're an arsehole who charges five euros fifty for a Perrier!" My friend was right, I shouldn't have called him an arsehole. He got angry and told me that he wasn't used to being spoken to like that and if I wasn't happy I should go elsewhere. He wasn't looking for a fight. Too bad, I was, and wouldn't have said no to a small tussle. Do *you* think it's okay to charge for a piece of lemon in a glass of water?

I should take up boxing again, to let off some steam. You could say I have mitigating circumstances. I work my socks off and when I get home, my mother is there waiting for me. She's a real sweetie and easy going, but she has her own home to go to. I'll end up taking it out on her if I don't calm down. I don't know how I'd cope without her. I need to get myself organized and contact the nursery again. I'm fed up with having to deal with everything while Juliette's head is all messed up—this is what's bugging me. I'd better stop before I say something I regret. I'm going to a friend's house near Fontainebleau next weekend with Adele; it'll do us both good.

You seem to want to know what we're supposed to do with our free time. Are you serious, John? Isn't it obvious? Nothing . . . Mope around, wallow in regret. We should tell ourselves, like you do, that there's no point changing because without love our existence has no meaning. That's it, isn't it?

And that it's better to carry on throwing our life away bored shitless in planes and firing people who haven't met their stupid targets. Sounds like a plan, John!

I'm sure you could negotiate your way out with a massive pay off. Not like those poor beggars you fire and give a few crumbs to by way of compensation. Why don't you help me open a community-sponsored restaurant and vegetable garden with the mentally disabled? On my own I just tend to procrastinate. You're quite right, I didn't think of you as the sentimental sort. It almost makes me laugh when I think of the pictures I've seen of you resembling a pit bull with that miserable mug of yours and the caption: "We must cut production costs." What a poetic soul you are . . .

See you later, alligator,
Nicolas

P.S. If I want to address Esther in my letters, I will.

GUILT

Jean to Juliette

Verjus-sur-Saône, 12th March 2019

Dear Juliette,

    Last weekend I had an impromptu visit from a former student, Julie, a concert pianist in Berlin. She must have been ten years old when I gave her her first lessons, and twenty-two when she joined the Paris Orchestra. She was a student at the Lyon Music Academy and took lessons from me at the weekend. She was gifted and hard-working but always went to pieces during exams. A few hours before an exam, she had eczema, nausea and would start to tremble. It was awful to witness. She had tried everything from psychotherapy and yoga to essential oils, relaxation and painkillers . . . I offered to help her. I had some experience, as I had already been a teacher for several years by then. I would keep her company in the hours leading up to her audition, right until the last minute. Together we would do whatever she wanted, except play the piano. She always chose walking. We would meet on the banks of the river Saône and walk briskly along the quays for two or three hours. Sometimes, when she was summoned early in the morning, we would meet there at dawn. While walking, we would talk about conductors, musicians and composers, and the lives of Chopin, Rachmaninoff, Beethoven, and Rimsky-Korsakov. We would discuss the era in which they were born, their families, love affairs, their first taste of success, their inspirations, their dark periods, and their moments of doubt . . . Anything except her exam. I would slip in words of encouragement: "At Pleyel that day, Chopin played the *Andante spianato*, which you played so well last week", "That's when Beethoven wrote his fugues, most likely to compete with Bach's *Goldberg Variations*. Do you remember how hard the No. 32 was for you? It was worth it though, wasn't it? Do me a favour, think about playing it for me next week, you play it better than I do." Then we would walk through the door of the Academy together. It worked. Our conversations had distracted her, and walking had given her a chance to relieve her stress and clear her head. You mentioned in your last letter that you learned from your staff. I learned from my students.

Best regards,
Jean

Juliette to Jean

Malakoff, 13th March 2019

Hello Jean,

When my daughter was born, my gynaecologist was surprised I didn't hold her close to me. So I promptly did so. Now I can tell him why. I didn't hold Adele because it never occurred to me to hold her. I have asked myself many times since what I was thinking at that moment. Well, nothing. My mind was blank. A total black out, disconnected from reality and the slightest emotion. I was unable to process that I had a child, that I was a mother.

While I was pregnant, I felt ugly, fat, bloated, red faced and puffy with swollen arms and legs. I lazed around and worried about everything and anything. Those nine months seemed like a lifetime, I couldn't wait for the baby to arrive. Adele was born at six in the morning. I gave her to the midwives the very first night. I was desperate to sleep. I had decided that I wouldn't breastfeed her. During the day, I felt awkward and fake in the role. I didn't know what to do with the baby and panicked when she wouldn't stop crying. I just wanted someone to come and take her from me for the night so I could sleep. In the morning, I was surprised to see her brought back so early. "What, already?" I thought to myself. I looked at my daughter and marvelled at her beauty, her fair skin, her dark blue eyes, her messy black hair, but it was as if her beauty was nothing to do with me. She was a burden to me already. All I wanted was to place her in her crib and for her to leave me alone. I hoped it would get better when we were home. But it got worse. Every day I came a bit closer to the cliff edge and I was the only one who could see it.

I was unable to cope with my daughter's crying. I tried to calm her down, but to no avail. I couldn't relate to her. I couldn't understand the look in her eyes, I didn't feel anything for her when I held her. A gulf opened up between us. The first few days at home, while she napped, I would wait impatiently for her to wake up. A few moments without her beside me, and I began to hope again. She would wake up and I would feel immense joy. Everything would be easy and picture book happy. We would forget those first few wasted days. Alas. I only had to look at her and take her in my arms when she woke up, and I was gripped by anxiety. I forced myself to cuddle and talk to her, but it was a lost cause. I felt empty inside. I did my duty. I fed her, bathed her, and changed her. But I did it all mechanically. I made a list for myself with schedules in case I forgot certain tasks. I was afraid of doing it wrong. In fact, I was terrified of forgetting her. I was so tempted to pretend she didn't exist. I felt no connection to my daughter.

She cried more and more. I was tired, anxious, on edge. Nicolas couldn't do anything right in my eyes. I was angry at him for leaving me alone with her, and I was jealous of the time he spent with her when he got back from work. He was overjoyed, worried about me, but delighted to be with her. I wanted Nicolas and I to get back to how we used to be. I wanted our baby to stop interfering in our relationship. I wished that she had never come between us.

It was becoming harder and harder to get out of bed and go outside in the street. Adele was two months old when Nicolas asked me why I didn't see a doctor. I accepted, without saying a word, but took it badly as it was confirmation that I had a screw loose, that I was going insane. The stigma was slowly killing me.

My GP prescribed vitamins and a low dose of sleeping pills to help me sleep. He sought to reassure me that I had done the right thing in coming to see him. The baby blues were not to be taken lightly, but I would soon forget about them. I came away feeling disappointed. I didn't want to go home. I wanted to go straight to a hospital or a clinic. I wanted to be taken care of and stuffed full with sleeping pills. I wanted to forget everything. The pain got worse. I was panicking all the time and found myself less and less able to take care of Adele. I stayed in my room, with my head under the duvet to drown out her cries. I would force myself to get up and feed her. I was afraid of hurting her. I kept telling myself that I was a monster. I was suffering from what the doctors call psychotic decompensation; my mind unleashed delusional fantasies and paranoia. I saw myself throwing Adele out the window in a moment of exasperation or smothering her gently under a pillow, then not daring to lift it to see her face afterwards. Or slitting my veins in the bathtub, slowly losing consciousness, the water turning dark red, and feeling cold.

I ended up in a psychiatric institution. It was what I wanted. To be taken care of, away from this baby that had devoured me, that I saw as a threat, but whom at the same time I wanted to protect from my madness. I wanted to be drugged up to the eyeballs. Adele was five months old. I stayed at the Sainte-Anne clinic for six weeks. I didn't want to see her. Not her, not anyone. No visits. I was done in. Even recalling this period is an ordeal for me.

Then I was transferred to a maternity unit. Adele would be with me several days a week. It was the first glimpse of light in the dark tunnel. The nursing staff understood me. They helped me, encouraged me to talk to my daughter, to touch her and sing to her. They encouraged me to rest. Every other day I spoke to a psychiatrist. I still didn't feel anything for my baby, but I wasn't panicking any more. There was no TV or radio, it was perfect. Calm and silence reigned, I wanted nothing more. Nicolas came to visit me. The only visit I finally allowed. I returned to our flat gradually at first, then for good. I only lasted a month. Nicolas did what he could. We were less tense around each other, but we couldn't communicate let alone love one another. I had to admit that he was avoiding me. I couldn't believe it. I was devastated by his attitude. I've been blaming him ever since. It wouldn't have taken much for me to get a little confidence back. He didn't do anything to help this. Our connection had gone, we were incapable of showing each other any affection. I didn't like the way he looked at me. I was terrified I might relapse. My panic attacks returned. I told my doctor and decided to leave. I wasn't ready.

I can't change what has happened. I can't make it right again.

Best,
Juliette

John to Esther

Paris, 16th March 2019

Hello Esther,

Now that you have told me about the correspondence you had with your father, I can see why you set up this workshop. Although I haven't yet said it, I'm delighted to be a part of it. Writing to you and Nicolas forces me to "step out of my comfort zone". (A rather fashionable expression, I believe.) It isn't easy. Memories resurface, I'm consumed with guilt and disturbed by your questions, which make me see things from a different angle. Is this the case for all of us, or just me?

I was in Paris for a good part of the week. I took the opportunity to have lunch with my parents. They are old: eighty-five and eighty-six. They both have their fair share of ailments and weaknesses. But overall, they are in good health. My father seemed happy to see me. He was more affectionate than usual. "Affectionate" is an exaggeration, but it was something along those lines. After I left them, I thought about my mother for a long while. (A consequence of the workshop, probably.) I admire her in a way. You can disapprove of her idea of happiness, and consider her stupid and immoral. But by marrying into money she fulfilled her dream of becoming wealthy and succeeded in preserving her well-being and defending what she believed in till the end: looking after her children as little as possible, enjoying her money without having to work, and donning the gowns and dresses favoured by the rich bourgeoisie. My mother read very little, didn't go to the cinema, rarely went to the theatre and didn't listen to music. She loved throwing dinner parties. A cook was in charge of the menus. What she liked most of all was to buy things. Clothes, jewellery, furniture, but also houses in the country or at the seaside, which she soon tired of. I can't say how many second homes they had. My father complied with her wishes, and my goodness there were many. He was weak. I felt sorry for him, even pity. In return, she never had a kind word to say about him. The worst thing is that she still nags and bullies him at eighty-five years old. My mother was stupid and beautiful. But she was happy.

As I mentioned in my letter, my work gave me immense pleasure and power. This is no longer the case, hence my use of the past tense. Did anything specific occur to bring about this indifference? If so, I don't remember what. I would be lying to you if I told you that the world's inequalities and misery bother me. Or that I feel guilty about all the people I've fired. Or that I'm remorseful and have decided to change my life. No, I'm more like one of those spoiled brats who don't know what to ask for on their birthday. Money doesn't give me a thrill any more, doesn't excite me. In these conditions, doing business is incredibly boring. In fact, I no longer do business as such. I manage human resources, people whose performance I evaluate and whom I discard when they don't perform well enough or cost too much. The fact that they are over fifty, have children, are ill, or that their spouse has left them is not my problem. They are mere pawns; I'm not a charity. I'm the one who has to give them the bad news, tell them that HR will call them within the week to settle the terms of their departure. I've become downright despicable. And I'm more and more demotivated every day. There's no going back. People have simply come and gone in my life. I don't have a wife any more. My children have no regard for me and have grown up, and I was never there for them (or hardly ever) anyway. My friends have forgotten me. The only thing I know in life is how to work.

To stop would be to jump off a cliff into a void. Yet I'm starting to consider it.

Tell me more about yourself, Esther. You're married, you have a daughter, Pia. How old is she? I'm so wrapped up in myself that I didn't even ask you.

I'm leaving for Brussels the day after tomorrow.

Best wishes,
John

Esther to John

Lille, 20th March 2019

Good evening John,

First, let me congratulate you. Your last letter wasn't awash with adverbs and your writing style was clearer and more concise as a result. I am delighted when I see that my advice is bearing fruit.

The question you must ask yourself is whether you can imagine yourself doing the same thing for the next fifteen years? Ten or twenty years from now, I will still be as happy as Larry running my bookshop and spending my days there. With all due respect, what you are experiencing is quite common. You're in your fifties, you're bored in your job and you don't know how to tackle the next part. Easy, either you put the cat among the pigeons or you grin and bear it? Why are we scared to confront ourselves? We are terrified of a void, having nothing and all those unanswered questions. We tell ourselves we must have a project at all costs, something, anything. However, I believe that we have to "jump off the cliff into the void", as you put it, to make it to the other side. Some people can't stand being where they are and yet they still don't know where they want to go. And they find it so hard to give the process the time it needs without freaking out! This is obviously what's happening to you, if what you wrote to me and Nicolas is anything to go by. No offense, as I don't wish to compare what you wrote to me with what you wrote to him, which I've read. But I agree with him that not wanting to change your life because you're on your own is a lame excuse. When we take risks, when we push back the boundaries, we discover hidden resources that we could never have imagined. As you can gather, I'm an advocate of putting the cat among the pigeons!

If I based my judgement merely on the content of your letters, logic dictates that I should brand you insufferable. Yet for some reason I can't. I don't know why. You represent everything I normally shun.

Pia is fifteen years old. Since she was born, I've been preparing myself for her teenage rebellion, yet there's no sign of it. Or let's say that the disruption is minimal. She stares at herself in every mirror that crosses her path (which exasperates me), is interested in boys (which makes me giggle), and is less bothered about reading than when she was younger (which devastates me). She is a top student and couldn't care less. She is smart, very funny, talkative and proud. Her grandfather's suicide really affected her, but she is better now. Her father and I are separated, but we get along well. We are friends now. He is a cinematographic sound engineer. He goes back and forth to Paris a lot. He works it so that he has his daughter at his place every other week. Neither he nor I have remarried or found new partners. I rarely meet someone I like. When I do, I soon spot their flaws and end it as soon as possible. I alternate between "I'm sick of being on my own" and "Isn't it nice to be able to do what you want at home without a guy around". I'm relatively happy in so far as my lifestyle suits me and

I'm living according to my principles and what I like doing. That's not to be scoffed at.

Best regards,
Esther

Nicolas to Juliette

Paris, 17th March 2019

My love,

My mother thinks you don't look too well again. You hardly said two words to her the day before yesterday. I'm worried. Talk to me.

When was the last time I called you "my love"? Words I adored saying as much as you adored hearing them. I'm curious to know what you are feeling as you read these words. I don't want our love to wane. I want it to regain its strength and vigour.

When you were at Sainte-Anne's, I didn't tell you, but I called your parents to put them in the picture and to invite them to come and see Adele. You can't imagine how guilty I felt. They hadn't seen her since they came to the hospital just after you'd given birth. In the meantime, you had cut ties with them, and I couldn't stomach the situation any longer. I remember them coming from Saint-Nazaire in their Sunday best to meet their granddaughter for the first time. Both of them had tears in their eyes; your mother with her suitcase full of presents which she had been accumulating for months, and your father standing proudly in his new suit, his hands clutching a bouquet of flowers and a bottle of lukewarm champagne. The memory made me weep. And I'm still weeping. I've always loved your parents,

Juliette, since the day I met them. Do you remember? It was in that fish restaurant near Trouville, on the coast. I can't remember its name. Your mother refused to cook saying she wouldn't be able to compete with me. They were dressed up to the nines that day too. Not like us. We had just come back from a long walk on the beach, looking scruffy in our jeans and muddy trainers like two ruffians.

Anyway, I called them. I gave them the run down, explaining what postpartum depression is. I apologized for not being available, despite knowing how worried they were when they called me trying to figure out what was going on. I thought that it was up to you to keep them in the picture. Your mother was worried about you and the baby but ultimately not that surprised. "It was only a matter of time before—" she said, without elaborating further. She asked me many questions about Adele. I learned in passing that my mother sent them photos regularly, which she had failed to mention to me. Sometimes I wonder whether she is afraid of my reactions or doesn't want to rock the boat. They think she looks just like you. "Even the eyes. Oh yes, the spitting image of her mother." They were supposed to call me back asap to tell me whether they were coming to Paris or not. I thought they would jump at the chance. Your father called me back the next day. After much thought, they decided that they would wait till you returned, and that it had to come from you. "It's our way of telling Juliette that we love her and respect what she's going through," they said. Since then, we've been phoning each other regularly.

Your daughter is a little piggy. Apart from leeks, which she turns her nose up at, she likes everything. She's landed in the right place with me and my mother. I won't try her on cake until you get back. We'll stick with savoury and leave the sweet stuff to you. She loves standing up and moves from one piece of furniture to another without tiring (unlike me!). I rarely give her a bath during the week, but love to do it at the weekend. Her rolls of flesh are so sweet, her skin is so soft and I adore that mischievous look she has when her hair is wet and plastered to her head. It cracks me up. She doesn't sleep enough, however, and wakes up a lot. But she doesn't do this when she has been in the maternity ward with you. Before you say "that doesn't mean a thing", hear me out. After our daughter has spent time with you, she sleeps more deeply and more peacefully. Probably because you have communicated, looked at each other and touched each other. She needs that connection.

N.

P.S. The nursery we applied to can take Adele from June. I'm in favour of it. It'll be good for her to mix with other children.

Juliette to Nicolas

Malakoff, 26th March 2019

Nicolas,

I'm sorry I took so long to answer you. The last few sessions with my therapist were difficult. I seemed to regress and I went back into my shell.

I had erased my birth from my timeline, pretending it was nothing out of the ordinary. I was a child like any other. I had the perfect childhood with parents as loving as Anne and Maxime, and only ever saw the glass as half full. If asked "given up at birth?", I would have replied "it's in the past, let's draw a line under it." If I had been more aware of who I was, of my strengths and weaknesses, I would have acted differently and understood that before giving birth, I had to make peace with my own birth first. I was in such denial that even when I was pregnant I didn't make any connection between being abandoned at birth and my distress. It took Adele to trigger the cycle. My therapist tells me that I unconsciously refused to let her carry the burden, which is good. I hope she's right.

I'm glad you called my parents. I'm relieved and touched to know that they are not mad at me and are waiting for me to return.

I don't want you to blame yourself, Nicolas, but I am trying to fathom out your attitude when I came out of the psychiatric hospital. Why were you so distant? You hardly spoke to me, you slept on the sofa, and you were so cold. It hurt like hell. Why did you do that? I needed your reassurance and support at that time more than ever. Without your love how could I hope to get back to my normal self? Please explain, even if it hurts me. I guess it's a good thing that Adele will go to nursery. At the clinic, she reaches out to the other children. They are encouraging me to be involved in her nursery induction, so I'll try.

My psychiatrist has reduced my antidepressants. I am taking small steps forward with her. I sometimes cry my eyes out like a little girl. And I vent my anger against my birth mother who didn't want me and didn't leave me a single memento. This stranger is someone I hate, but who inevitably occupies a tiny (very tiny) space in my life. It makes me happy to know you are waiting till I'm back before giving Adele any cake. For the first time, I can imagine myself at home in the kitchen, baking her little cupcakes and choux puffs. Why didn't I think of bringing her sweet things when I come to pick her up? How lame of me.

Alex and Joel called me this morning. They are thinking of buying an old mill in the Brie region. They want me to partner with them. We would make our own flours using traditional millstones and develop the business. We wouldn't start from scratch as the current owners already have a good client base. It would be up to us to do what it takes to keep them. Everything is organic. Rather than opening a third bakery as we discussed, I prefer this idea. It would be a real challenge. What do you think?

I often reminisce about when we first met, and how happy we were all those years. I ruined everything.

With much love and affection,
Juliette

Juliette feels better for writing this letter. Maybe this workshop is a good thing. Maybe she and Nicolas will be able to talk things through. In their panic, hurt and anger, they said painful and regrettable things to each other, until one day, after weeks of arguments and misunderstandings, they stopped communicating altogether. Juliette hardly left her bed. Nicolas slept on the sofa in the living room, and avoided her. She discovered a new talent of his: fleeing reality. This was too much for her to bear. What she prized most about him was his honesty and spontaneity. Such loyalty was priceless. Regrettably, she had got it all wrong. He was doing his utmost to avoid her and avoid confrontation. Such cowardly, mean behaviour was intolerable to her.

Once Juliette had gone, there was a gaping hole, which took them both by surprise and affected them quicker than they would have thought possible. They knew their relationship was hanging by a thread. They knew they had to show leniency to one another and overlook the shouts, the insults, and the snide and hurtful remarks and behaviour. One step over the line would signal the end of their relationship. It was obvious they loved each other, but love no longer seemed enough to hold the fragile relationship together. Juliette had to be honest about her feelings towards Nicolas if they were to re-establish any sort of dialogue. Yes, she felt hatred towards her mother-in-law who had taken her place. Juliette was one big contradiction and she still considered herself *incapable*. She chose her words carefully. She knew what she was saying and took full responsibility for the harshness of her words, but what choice did she have? After grappling with the inertia and fear of the first few months, she was now battling her rage.

Jean to Samuel

Verjus-sur-Saône, 20th March 2019

Dear Samuel,

Borrowing your brother's books to take up reading is a super initiative. He will be your guide. Perhaps while he was alive, he would have enjoyed such a role. I understand that you are concerned about the place you now occupy in your family. The answer wasn't even clear when your brother was around. Of course, your place would have been different if he hadn't been ill. But that's the way it is and there's nothing you can do about it. Samuel, you seem to think that your parents love you less, or that you no longer exist for them since your brother died. Do you love your parents less? I doubt it, but you see them differently. They had two children, now they have only one. There were four of you, now there are only three. The family unit has been turned upside down. It will adjust in time but will be different. Your parents are devastated by the loss. They no longer know what to say or do. Do you not think that like you they are afraid of doing the wrong thing?

Ah, time is not always on our side, Samuel, but in your case it is. Be patient, and use this time to read!

And do me a favour please. Stop feeling guilty! You wanted your brother's room back and you wished he would disappear because he was the centre of attention and a constant source of worry for you and your parents. You wanted it to end once and for all. Your reaction is only human. You did not hasten his death. Or maybe you are superhuman and possess extraordinary powers I don't know about?

I read *Reunion* years ago. It's a book you won't forget, and a classic too. Have you finished it?

Jean

Samuel to Jean

28th March

Hello Jean,

I really liked *Reunion*. Obviously when you're talking to someone who hasn't read it, you mustn't spoil the ending, but I thought it was brilliant. The worst part is when the parents who so loved, admired and had faith in their German homeland gassed themselves.

I'm Jewish too, but not practising. We don't talk about religion at home. We just have a mezuzah in the hallway.

I've just finished *Nagasaki* by Eric Faye, the second book on the shelf. Nothing like *Reunion*, but I liked it. I don't know if you've read it, so I'll just tell you the beginning. It's an eerie story, based on true life apparently. It's about a depressed meteorologist in Japan who installs a webcam in his flat because someone breaks in to eat a yogurt and drink tea . . . What I liked best was the strange, slightly surreal atmosphere like you're in a dream. And also that the man ends up no longer feeling at home as he knows what happened there and the role he plays in the events that follow. But I won't tell you the rest in case you decide to read it one day. I can now see that my brother didn't like happy stories. He only kept his favourite books in his room and left the others on the bench outside. When he couldn't do it himself, he would ask me to take them down. Julian had some strange habits. If a book disappointed him, it had to go. I need to read *For Whom the Bell Tolls* by Ernest Hemmingway next, but it's a bit daunting as it's very long.

I can't wait for next Tuesday. Me and my friend Ben are going to see a cabaret act in Paris. I don't know them but his sister is a big fan. She gave him two tickets for his birthday. I used to go to Paris on Saturdays but stopped. My parents don't give me pocket money any more. My father got my back up not long ago. He said I had to think about what I wanted to do, that this was the last year I would stay at home bumming around like this. He suggested I make an appointment with the careers advisor at his school. I agreed. But they're all blockheads, careers advisors. Though I kind of liked that he was worried about me.

I dream about Julian almost every night. It's always the same dream. We're about ten and twelve years old. We are walking in a meadow, holding hands. It's a beautiful day. We are dressed the same, in brown shorts, white T-shirts, hiking boots and a backpack. The grass is short, and there are no trees, no flowers, only a lawn that goes on forever. You can't see the end of it. I don't know where we are heading but pretend I do. The more we walk, the higher the grass gets. When it reaches our chests, we have to lift our legs higher to keep going. There are trees. They get taller and taller and block out the sunlight. We cross a forest of fir trees. I ask myself since when have there been fir trees all around us? And why didn't I notice them before? The forest is getting thicker and thicker. We follow a path that becomes so narrow that I let go of my brother's hand and take the lead. The brambles scratch me, but I only have to touch my hand to make the scratches disappear. Julian stumbles. I turn around, and wait for him to get up. He's in pain. His face, legs and arms are scratched. He falls once, twice, three times. He gets up without complaining. The path has come to an end. Too bad, I keep going. When I turn around, my brother has gone. I realize that I haven't turned around for a while and that I'm walking without him. I forgot him, he is way behind me. It's over. I wake up. If I told my ex-therapist he would probably say: "Interesting, Samuel. What do you think?" And I would reply, "That I'm an arsehole for being alive."

Samuel

That Sunday morning, at the bistro, Jean got into an argument with Luc. When she arrived, she noticed the smug, proud look on his face. He had spent the whole of Saturday at the Les Vignes roundabout with the other members of the local Yellow Vests campaign group, blocking the main road and handing out sweets to motorists. Jean had known about this in advance. She had decided not to go to Villeurbanne the day before, lest she be stranded there. Luc proudly handed her the local paper, *Le Progrès*. There was a photo of them wrapped up in their anoraks, posing for the camera, and standing around a stove. Jean shrugged and rolled her eyes. "You screw up people's journeys and hand them sweets in return. Is that all you can come up with? Frankly, when I see you lot sat around your bonfires, it's like looking at a bunch of stupid kids at summer camp." The conversation had got out of hand, and things got a little heated. Luc ridiculed her fight against the property developers as "a rich man's problem". And then how could she possibly understand the Yellow Vests' grievances when she had her "comfortable pension to live on"? Jean can relate to some of their demands but finds it unacceptable to stop people getting to work. Not to mention those in cities who smash windows, destroy bus shelters and set fire to rubbish bins. "It's the only way to get our voices heard," shouted Luc. Jean retorted that he should be ashamed of himself.

John to Nicolas

Paris, 24th March 2019

Hello Nicolas,

In my last letter I wrote that I'm finding it difficult to project myself into the future, notably because I'm on my own. I'm not complaining about it, yet you're not listening to what I'm saying. I almost quit writing to you and then I reconsidered. I mean we don't have to see eye to eye, do we? You gave the man with the lemon slices a hard time, and I paid the price too, as it were. I agree it's objectionable to charge for a slice of lemon, but in all honesty, I wouldn't have checked the bill before paying (I know this will annoy you). God knows how many lemon slices I must have forked out for in my life.

You imply that it would be easy for me to just drop everything and wait and see what life throws at me because I have money. It's not that simple. I mean you're still in Paris, even though you want to leave at times. I've worked hard to get where I am. I have devoted twenty years of my life to it. My work is all I'm good at, do you see that?

Now let's change the subject. My kids both went to top business schools. Boris works for the telecoms operator Orange. He likes it there. If I didn't call him when I'm in Paris, I'd never see him. We always meet at a restaurant. He tells me about his job, I tell him about mine, and our laborious discussion ends there. We are both relieved when the bill arrives. He has put a brick wall between us. I assume he resents me for not being there for him when he was a child. I can understand that. Deep down, he must know that I didn't want to be a father. I should be brave and tell him one day. But I can't as I don't regret being who I was. So I keep quiet. Things would be different if I could genuinely tell him that if I had to do it all over again I would behave differently. Or that I sacrificed part of my personal life so that he and his sister would never want for anything. But that would be a lie. I did it all for me and me alone.

Emma is acquisitions manager at Vente-privee.com. She told me last week that she wanted to quit her job and study literature or take a creative writing class. Deep down I'm not displeased about this. I asked her for what purpose she wants to do a degree in literature. She didn't know exactly, but when I insisted she stammered: "I want to write." I hugged her, kissed her, and congratulated her. She wasn't expecting me to react like this. When Emma was young, she excelled at French. At the time I was sorry that she had chosen business studies over literature. But given that I forgot to ask her about her Baccalaureate results, I kept my head down and avoided giving her my opinion. Which, by the way, she didn't even ask me. Just because she had top marks in French doesn't mean she'll be a talented writer. The new path she has chosen promises to be exciting. Difficult, but exciting. Her mother is furious; she thinks it's a mistake. Emma was tearful. I don't understand why at twenty-five years old she is still swayed by her mother's opinion. Why didn't she remind her mother that her second husband is an artist? I held my tongue. (Again? you might ask.)

I leave for Chicago in the morning. I'm attending a symposium on e-waste recycling. I hope to find a moment to visit the Art Institute. Yes, that's right, on my own.

John

P.S. How is your *je ne sais quoi* coming along?

Nicolas to John

Paris, 31st March 2019

Hello John,

You're right; you also bore the brunt of my bad mood. I do apologize. The truth is, without my wife around I act like a jerk.

Whether she succeeds or not, what your daughter Emma is doing is positive. She has found her calling. That's the kind of decision you can't regret.

You don't come across as very warm or expressive with your children. I gather you don't ever show them how you really feel. You're delighted for your daughter, but all you can say is: "I'm not displeased about this". And you ask her "for what purpose" she wants to do a degree in literature. "For what purpose?" It sounds like a conversation between a boss and his employee . . . Then you suddenly switch from astonishment to joy, and start hugging her. And you're surprised that she is surprised? How many times have you rejoiced in front of your daughter? How many times have you spontaneously hugged her? If you answer this question you'll understand her amazement. I bet she was scared to tell you the news, especially after her mother's reaction. I'm right aren't I? I'm usually good at this kind of guessing game. (Okay, not when it comes to my wife.) You're changing, John. You feel the need to express your thoughts. I hope I'm on the right track. If you ask me what I think, all I can say is that it's positive.

My menu will soon be featuring a springtime *je ne sais quoi* of asparagus with sea urchins, taramasalata and lemongrass.

See you later, alligator,
Nicolas

P.S. Does your daughter know you're participating in a writing workshop?

Nicolas to John

Paris, 1st April 2019

There's something I forgot to mention to you in my letter yesterday. You'll get this one the day after. I don't know anyone more uncommunicative and more uncivilized than my father. On Sunday mornings, he used to take me and my sister frog fishing. On the whole, he didn't like us talking much during these outings. He wasn't interested in our school marks. When, at the age of seventeen, I told him that I wanted to become a chef, he ruffled my hair and said: "Why not? That'd be nice", then went back to his stove. My mother was the opposite. She spoke enough for both of them. We couldn't walk past her without getting a big hug. She never changed. Our father was neither demonstrative nor affectionate; just like you. But my sister and I never doubted his love. We felt safe with him, like nothing could happen to us. No one would have contemplated messing with his wife or children. I grew up but he stayed the same.

The only one who dares push him around a bit is Juliette. She doesn't care that he doesn't respond to her affection. "Don't look *too* happy about it, Michel", she says in annoyance when she thinks he could show a little more enthusiasm. When she uses such a familiar tone with him, my heart stops. I never know how he'll take it. And then he inevitably smiles. He likes Juliette a lot. I know what he thinks of her. He approves of the fact that she is a baker because when you make bread, you tend to be down to earth. Not like his son with his head in the clouds, his fancy restaurant and his Michelin stars. He wasn't happy that I moved to Paris. He knew that it was Juliette's idea but, strangely enough, he quickly forgot about that detail. He never asks me any questions about the restaurant, or about my cooking. He half-heartedly congratulated me on my Michelin star, although my mother said he told everyone in Bourg-en-Bresse. She says he is proud of me but has a complex about it all. What rubbish! It's ridiculous and hurtful. His brasserie served traditional fare, which I think I already told you was excellent. And who made me want to become a chef in the first place? He did. Since Juliette left, he calls me every day. Did you hear that? Every day! And it's not a group call with his wife either. No, it's one on one, to talk to me. He talks about the weather in Bourg-en-Bresse, his vegetable garden, his dog walks, a new leak in the bathroom, the car he just bought, his computer that's riling him, and *Top Chef*. I talk about Camellia, Adele, my suppliers, what my mother and I are giving her to eat and so on. Every morning, I wait for his phone call. Knowing I can count on my father at forty years old and that he worries about me is a godsend.

One day, Boris will need you. There will be no grand explanation as to why or how. What you have left unsaid will continue to eat away at you. But when the time comes, you'll be there for him. That's all there is to it.

See you later, alligator,
Nicolas

ANIMAL

nico-esthover@free.fr, juju-esthover@free.fr,
jean.dupuis5@laposte.net, john.beaumont2@orange.com,
samsam-cahen@free.fr

Hello everyone,

As promised, here are the three exercises that I suggest you include in your next letters (you will all do them twice, since you are each writing to two people). The first two exercises are forms of speech: first a dialogue, then a monologue. Fiction or reality. For the third, you will have to use your imagination as we have jumped forward to the year 2029. What are you up to now?

You don't have to do them all at once. But please respect the order of dialogue, monologue, 2029. Finally, please indicate which exercise you're doing at the top of your letter.

Regarding the dialogue: the Larousse dictionary defines dialogue as "a conversation between two or more people on a specific subject; content of this conversation; an interview, or discussion." At least two people must be involved. Remember to alternate between direct and indirect speech, don't overuse verbs of dialogue attribution (he said, he stated, he asked), vary the length of your sentences, and the way your characters express themselves must reflect their personalities.

Georges Simenon, Agatha Christie and Ernest Hemingway mastered the art of written conversation perfectly. Before you start, I advise you to read some of their work.

Regarding the monologue: Édouard Dujardin (1861–1949) gave this definition in his book entitled *Le Monologue intérieur*: "A speech that has no audience and is not spoken aloud. It is the expression of the most intimate thoughts, those which lie nearest the unconscious; by its very nature it is a speech which precedes logical organization, reproducing the intimate thoughts just as they are born and just as they come; as for form, it employs direct sentences reduced to the syntactical minimum to give the impression of an unfiltered, naturally jumbled thought process.

You will find very beautiful interior monologues in Louis Aragon's *Aurélien*, Virginia Woolf's *The Waves*, William Faulkner's *The Sound and the Fury*, Natalie Sarraute's *Childhood*, and Albert Camus' *The Fall*.

For the last exercise, you have free rein.

These exercises are an opportunity to put into practice what you have learned in the workshop. Think about all the points we've discussed so far.

Jean to Juliette

Verjus-sur-Saône, 17th March 2019

Dear Juliette,

You cannot change what has happened. But you can fix it. You must accept your failings and live with them. Your daughter loves you as you are, warts and all. You are doing all you can to get better and I have the feeling your relationships are improving too. You will have hardly enjoyed the first few months of your daughter's existence. This is unfortunate, but life is long, and you have many years ahead of you. One day you'll tell her what happened to you.

I don't know the reasons behind your breakdown; maybe you don't either. But I have a feeling that if you dig deep, with honesty and courage, you will break the cursed chain. Motherhood has awakened a lot of pain in you. You broke down, only to rise again. I have read *Trembling Mothers*, by Maman Blues, an association of women who have had the same experience as you. I assume you've heard of it? It is a collection of real-life stories from victims of post-partum depression. They have all recovered. Today, they have a normal relationship with their child. Look what's happened to me. My daughter and I were extremely close for twenty-five years, and suddenly out of the blue, nothing. Not a single explanation. I could never have imagined such a thing; that it would have come to this. That I, her mother, who cherished, adored and nurtured her, would be incapable of forgiving her and protecting her. Am I abnormal? What sort of mother am I? What sort of father am I? These are questions that all parents ask themselves at some point in time. For me, it's every morning when I get up and every evening when I go to bed. I'm writing to young Samuel. I don't know if you remember him? I have a lot of affection for this lad, who looked so sullen at our meeting. I lied to Samuel and told him that I rarely see my daughter as she is married and living in China. I couldn't bring myself to tell him the truth, even though he opened up to me, saying he would never have children and how complicated his relationship with his parents is. Married and living in China? Why did I concoct such a story? It's a mystery . . . You wonder why your husband avoided you when you came out of hospital. Did you ask him?

Some good news came my way. I managed to get a meeting with the mayor and an architect who specializes in eco housing developments. He builds houses with wooden frames and straw walls. They are partly heated with solar energy, and have water butts for collecting rainwater, nice individual gardens, shared common rooms and vegetable plots. I hold the mayor in high esteem, notwithstanding our differences. He asked me why I was so attached to prehistory. He has a sense of humour alright. He has that in his favour at least. It's a pity that he is so disinterested in ecology and architecture. I asked him why we can't do here what's been done in Brittany and the north of France. He sighed, saying that it looks like I'll have the last word yet again. We made peace in his garden over a bottle of Beaujolais-Villages.

You'll be fine, Juliette.

Jean

Juliette to Jean

Malakoff, 29th March 2019

Hello Jean,

Thanks for your encouragement. It really helps me. Regarding your daughter, I feel both pity and admiration for you. Giving up trying to see her and no longer waiting to hear from her are courageous deeds. You're right, we don't have to accept everything our children throw at us. It must have been a terribly difficult decision to make. And to stick to it, even more so. I genuinely wonder whether you're doing the right thing in not trying to reconnect with her though.

You say that maybe I don't know what's behind my depression. I certainly do know and I thought I told you. I was given up at birth on 10th December 1979 in Caen. My mother didn't leave me anything, no letter of explanation, and not a single item to remind me of her. I was taken in by a couple who had applied to adopt a child eight years before. For them, I was the eighth wonder of the world. They showered me with love. I have wonderful parents. They didn't hide anything about my origins from me. It wasn't a taboo subject. I just tucked it away in a corner. When I thought about it, I only touched the surface of it casually, even flippantly. Was it my real father or my real mother who had dark hair, almond-shaped eyes, and full eyebrows? Searching never occurred to me. I didn't even know it was possible. I recently learned that there are specialized websites. You enter your name, and your place and date of birth, and they cross-reference that information with their database. There is also the National Council for Access to Personal Origins. The truth is, I don't want to know. I'm afraid what I might discover. It's too late. I would prefer to learn how to make a tiny space in my life for this shadow of a mother. I want to move forward with what has been taken from me and what has been given to me, having, as you so rightly say, broken the cursed chain.

You admired your husband. I admire mine too, for the way he has carved out his own path in life. Did I not tell you about him? His Michelin stars didn't go to his head, despite being proud of them. I was relieved to see that he has remained true to himself. It's not that he's indifferent to the invitations and the compliments that such awards elicit, it's just that it's like water off a duck's back to him. He always comes back to the root of his passion; just a kid amazed by the art of cooking. Paris could have robbed him of his high spirits and originality, but he refused to let this happen. Trendy restaurants exasperate him if the food isn't good, as do bistros that charge the earth. Nicolas gets indignant easily. He says what he thinks and can quickly fly off the handle. He likes to cause a scandal. When I see him getting angry,

I tell him to calm down and move on, but he doesn't see or hear me any more. He has only one desire: to rush in with all guns blazing. When this happens, my darling volcano drives me crazy.

You must come and dine at Camellia, Jean. The food is exquisite and the decor is beautiful. Nicolas has kept the original stone walls, and added a concrete floor. He chose thick, charcoal-coloured velvet curtains, smoked oak tables, and aged black leather chairs. His father remarked that it was "rather somber" when he dined there. And he's not wrong.

Well done for setting up a meeting with your mayor. Persistence pays off. I don't know much about green architecture. My parents live on a housing estate which is similar to the ones you describe.

Since this workshop began, Esther keeps pointing out to me that I have trouble with connections, and that I don't use coordinating conjunctions enough. I think about what she said before writing, then I forget; I can't seem to help myself. I hope that you can understand what I've written in spite of this.

Best regards,
Juliette

John to Esther

Canton–Paris, 27th March 2019

Hello Esther,

"You represent everything I normally shun." That sentence is enough to make anyone feel down in the dumps. A bit of compassion wouldn't go amiss. I bared my soul to you and Nicolas. Questioning oneself is never easy. You don't do things by halves do you? Dumping your boyfriends as soon as you "spot their flaws"? I'm curious to know what those flaws were to merit the death sentence.

I often think about you and your father. Or rather, the way you corresponded with one another. It's really rather rare.

If I give up working, I plan to spend my days on my balcony. That way I can observe the sky and gaze at the walkers and lovers who meet in the Tuileries gardens. I adore that place. This is where I see myself. The days will pass by and I'll become as stale as a six-pound loaf, as my grandmother would say. My brain refuses to project itself any further than this balcony and its view.

As it's you, Esther, I'll force myself to imagine the rest. It's winter, I'm shivering on my balcony wrapped in a blanket. I smoke not one, but two packs a day. I'm weary. I contemplate the passers-by: that gentleman and his dachshund at seven o'clock sharp every morning; the dog-sitter who walks briskly along with a dozen dogs at his heels; the joggers with headsets on their ears; nannies sitting on a bench chatting while the children play; the park sweepers and gardeners who work on the paths at all hours of the day; the tourists, who walk then stop and gawp like, well, tourists. Alas, there comes a point when they no longer entertain me. The time has come for me to leave without a trace. I am preparing to disappear. I'll evaporate like they do in Japan. I'll shed my skin, my name, become a different person, get rid of any constraints, any influence, and place no more demands on myself or on others. I'll become a nobody. Is this change radical enough, Esther?

Sincerely,
John

For fear of tarnishing his image further, John doesn't mention his work to Esther. Nor the ungracious task he has been asked to perform in recent years; a task he carries out without a second thought. Arnaud and Pascal preyed on his weakness—money. They gave him more and more donkey-work; the most unscrupulous tasks out there. John had no scruples. He would have accepted any mission, as long as it paid well. He used to think that Arnaud and Pascal considered him as a friend. He's no longer sure. At worst they despise him, and at best they're indifferent. He'd likely be the same in their shoes.

Esther to John

2nd April 2019

John,

You are unbelievable! I wrote that logic dictates I should avoid you like the plague but that for some reason I can't. And you accuse me of having no compassion, based on this one sentence: "You represent everything I normally shun." Your response does neither of us justice. You make me out to be some authoritarian shrew who discards men at the drop of a hat. You imagine I give them ultimatums such as "I don't like your voice, let's call it a day", or "That's funny, I hadn't noticed that you eat with your mouth open", or "If I'd known you drank herbal tea for breakfast, I wouldn't have stayed over last night." You're wrong. On the contrary, I'm careful to conceal my hang ups about relationships from them. I either pretend that I want to be on my own or that it's the wrong time to start a relationship.

Yes indeed, the way me and my father used to correspond was rather original. Yes, by writing to each other—especially

living in the same city—we resembled two whimsical dino-
saurs. Maybe it's because of my "letter-writing past" that
I can't get on with emails, texts or social media. On Instagram, where you share photos and videos, you don't need
words to display your ego. Beautiful locations, smiling faces,
tanned bodies, funny cats, appetizing meals and so on. At
best, you add a caption, just to make people laugh. I find it
offensive this one-upmanship, this fake and syrupy happiness, and this proud and smug narcissism. WhatsApp is no
better. You can no longer attend a dinner or a party, or go on
a weekend or holiday without creating a group and collect-
ively informing the entire world of your every move, backed
up by comments and photos, which are inevitably terrible.
Why can't we appreciate the present moment without cap-
turing it? Can't we just let it go? Why can't we appreciate
things and events for what they are? It's sheer overkill. When
I try to convince my daughter of the advantages of writing,
she merely tries to convince me of the advantages of social
media. She blames me for caricaturing and despising such
networks. She uses Instagram to show her work, share experiences, defend her opinions, and tell stories. She makes
me feel like I'm one hundred years old and out of it. And to
top it all, she uses all that social media speak. We always end
up arguing.

I know the Tuileries gardens, it's a beautiful park. You're
lucky to live across the road from it. What you say about
spending your days on the balcony sounds a bit exaggerat-
ed. And why do you talk about "evaporating"? In Japan you
evaporate and become a *johatsu* when you're laid off, or to
escape an anxiety-fuelled job, an unbearable family situation,
a debt, or a dishonour. Why would you want to disappear
without trace? I know you're joking but go easy on me please.
I've had my dose of men who write to me to tell me how
worthless their lives are. It's not my idea of a joke.

I decided to be courageous and brought home the letters I sent to my father for over twenty years. I knew he kept them in boxes, but I didn't know they were so neatly filed in chronological order. I have started to file his but am not done yet. My father was very disciplined, unlike me. I don't want to read them again, I'm not ready. I've only just noticed that my handwriting has changed in twenty years and now resembles his. Imagine the scene: I'm sat there in the middle of dozens of boxes with some six thousand letters scattered around me. That's how Pia found me, after spending a week at her father's house. She thought it was "pretty scary". She wants to know if she will ever be allowed to read them. She will, of course.

Best regards,
Esther

P.S. If you get the time, please send me a picture of your view of the Tuileries. On a rainy day, if possible. Or better still, in the fog!

Nicolas to Juliette

Paris, 30th March 2019

My sweet Juliette,

When you came home, I didn't know what to expect. I was terrified that you would break down again and become hysterical. It was all I could think about. I would call the doctor at the first sign of trouble. I didn't want any more of your criticizing, your despair, your madness, your jealousy. Before I put the key in the lock, I would take a deep breath and pray that I wouldn't find you in bed going insane. I was on edge and so tense. Exhausted from it all, I kept a low profile, hoping that you would get back on track, and start again from scratch with Adele. I would have loved to get away for a few days. I didn't give any thought to us getting back together again. I know you blame me for this. I couldn't do anything else. If you had said, "Tell me you love me, I need your reassurance, to get back my self-confidence", I couldn't have done it.

Do you remember the lyrics of that song, "Secret Dreams of a Prince and Princess", that you chose for our wedding ceremony? It was playing on the radio the other day.

So what are we to do with all this love?
Shall we show it or keep it hidden?
We'll do what's forbidden,
We'll have a drink or three,
We'll smoke a pipe secretly,
And we'll stuff ourselves with pastries.
But what are we to do with all these pleasures?
There are so many on this Earth . . .

It resembled us, this song. We liked to ask ourselves this question. What are we going to do with so much happiness? We seized it with both hands and tasted it each day, as if it was the first and the last. Fifteen years later, we were still telling ourselves that we had a little miracle on our hands. At least, I told myself that. Maybe I idealized us?

As I listened to the end of the song, I laughed, nervously. Listen:

We'll have lots of children, of course, and we'll never fail,
To live happily ever after in a charming fairy tale.

I don't care about having lots of children. I just want you to come back to me and for the three of us to smoke a pipe secretly and gorge ourselves on pastries. And everything would be just perfect.

N.

Juliette to Nicolas

Malakoff, 7ᵗʰ April 2019

Nicolas,

That song begins like this: *I didn't know you loved me.
Are you certain of it now?* I was afraid you didn't love me
any more. I can't make it on my own. Thank God I've got
your letters, full of tender loving words and encouragement.
I read them day and night. They delight and comfort me.
Yesterday, I went to the maternity unit with Adele, in better spirits than usual. And do you know what? We laughed
together for the very first time. This is what happened. We
were in the playroom when a little boy started to cry. She
stopped playing, looked at him and tried to imitate him. She
couldn't do it. She twisted her mouth, puffed up her cheeks
and squinted her eyes. She was so funny. I started to laugh
and couldn't stop. She looked at me in surprise and then
burst out laughing too, really loudly. It felt so good! I forgot
everything for a few minutes. The only thing that mattered
was laughing with her. I experienced my first moment of
true happiness with our daughter. It was sheer bliss, like
nothing I've ever experienced before. Adele cried when I
kissed her goodbye. I did too. I guess your mother already
told you? She shed a tear too and asked me why I didn't stay.
I didn't answer.

I hope there will be many more firsts with Adele and that
nothing is lost. This is the start of our lifelong journey together, though a bit later than expected. In my dreams, I'm
kissing you. I run my hand through your hair, you take me
in your arms and undress me, then I can't see you any more.
I'm naked and you've vanished.

You didn't say any more about your blandness theme.
Émeline told me that some new bakeries have opened up

on Rue des Martyrs. I had a look. I wonder how they sur-
vive. In one single street there are four bakeries, two patis-
series, a meringue place and a choux puff shop. Can you
believe it? The praline brioche is extremely popular at the
moment; I tasted one and it was nothing to write home
about. The pastry was good but the praline was too sweet.
It's always the same: either the praline is bad and they put
too much in, or it's good and you can count the pieces
on the fingers of one hand. This has given me the idea of
a flaky brioche with cappuccino. We're seeing more and
more organic and artisan flours around, which is encouraging for my mill project. At last I'll have the opportunity
to produce and select my own flours. I've noticed things
are not as rigid as they used to be; the use of unlisted grains
seems to be on the increase.

I did attempt to write to my parents but I couldn't do it.

With much love and affection,
Juliette

Jean to Samuel

Verjus-sur-Saône, 1st April 2019

Dear Samuel,

When I next go to Lyon, I'll buy *Nagasaki*. I read *For
Whom the Bell Tolls* when I was sixteen. I remember because
at the time I was dating a Spanish lad in my class. Jesús. I
knew it was a common name in his country. But for me,
raised in an atheist family, it was quite extraordinary to be
called that. How does one live with the name of a prophet?
What sort of parents would choose to name their son Jesus?
I stared at him not knowing the answers, but soon fell in love

with him. My Jesús (pronounced "Rrrézusse") didn't care much about the real Jesus and all the rest of his crowd. *He* was passionate about the Spanish War.

It's great that you are persevering with the books. Have your parents noticed? You hadn't told me about your friend Ben until now. Have you known each other long?

I rarely remember my dreams. My husband on the other hand loved to tell me his. They were amazing. "And then?" I would ask when he abruptly stopped talking. "That's it. It stops there," he would say. Yours are clear, they have a beginning, a middle and an end. And no, you're not an arsehole. The next time you go for a walk in the forest, turn around and say goodbye to your brother, who can't go on and for whom you can't do anything.

I haven't forgotten to tell you about my animals but didn't know where to start. I hope you will share my empathy for them, or at least respect it. I'm afraid you'll think I'm ridiculous. The best thing is to tell you how I became so devoted to them. For my thirtieth birthday, Hadrian, my husband, gave me a dog. His name was Sunday. He was a flat-coated retriever. He was tall, lithe and muscular, with black eyes and long black fur. Flat-coated retrievers are beautiful dogs, and he was a particularly fine specimen. He was intended to have been a guide dog but didn't meet their criteria and was put up for adoption at eighteen months old. He had a lovely nature and bags of energy. It made Hadrian and me laugh to imagine him as a guide dog. The poor blind man or woman would have ended up flat on their back in the gutter with a dog like him!

Sunday died at the age of ten. His last few months were tough. He had cancer in his hip. He loved to run and swim, but every day he went more and more downhill. You should have seen him running in the woods or walking on the ice when the pond was frozen! It gradually became impossible, however, and our walks got shorter and shorter. He would sit in the middle of the road waiting till he felt strong enough to stand up. I would sit next to him and stroke him. "We're not in a hurry," I used to say. It wasn't true. I had appointments; I was late. He would get up and we would walk on, one step at a time. I tried to stay behind him, to make him feel that he was still leading me, as he had always done. He couldn't bear to walk behind Hadrian or me. Sunday didn't have a leash. I have a hard time with leashes, muzzles, cages, whips, bits and so on; all that paraphernalia restricts an animal's freedom and merely embodies humans' domination over them. I used to tell him how courageous he was as we walked along. It hurt me to say it, but I thought it. Until then I had looked down on old people who talk to their dogs in the street. My brave boy was suffering, but he wouldn't concede defeat. When I said to him: "Shall we go for a walk?" he would suddenly get up, wobbling on his legs and trying not to fall over. I was afraid he would collapse. The cancer spread to his liver, then to his lungs. We could only take a few steps along the pavement before going home to lay him down. He got so thin and weak.

We put off the dreaded moment several times. But one morning he wouldn't get up. He appeared to be in a lot of pain. It was the end. I wanted him to die at home. I called the vet. I petted him, laid down next to him, put my head against his, and talked to him while sobbing: "You are a wonderful dog, Sunday. You are the dog I have always dreamed of having since I was a little girl." I dreaded the sound of the doorbell. It finally rang. The vet put him down and he died peacefully.

I spent twelve days crying from morning to night, Samuel. It was unimaginable. My tears wouldn't stop. Crying like that, non-stop for a long time, is exhausting. Everything reminded me of Sunday. I missed him all the time. I would open the door to my flat, and he wouldn't be there to greet me. I would get in the car and I wouldn't see his beautiful face in the middle of the rear-view mirror. I had a memory of him in every street, shop and park. I was totally distraught, to the point of being ashamed. I couldn't talk about it. I lacked the words. If I had told my friends how grief stricken I was, they would have deemed it disproportionate and ridiculous. Even indecent. I knew I would get over it, that wasn't the problem. I just didn't understand the intensity of my grief, why I couldn't control it. I had lost a dog, not a child. I had been preparing for the worst for a while now. So, what happened? My theory is that the relationship between man and dog is unique, and incomparable. A dog is totally and utterly devoted to his master as if it were his whole life. He has only one goal: to satisfy him. He is loyal, affectionate and loves his master unconditionally. If I had been cruel to Sunday, hit him, starved him, terrorized him, he would have looked up at me with sad, doleful eyes, but he would still have remained faithful and docile, until his last breath. I can't help but have total admiration for such steadfast loyalty and love. Beyond that, there is something staggering about it. With Sunday I became aware how easy it is to take advantage of a dog and his kindness, and to treat him with contempt and indifference. (I'm not talking about people who mistreat animals here.) To make him bear the brunt of our bad mood, to not walk him when we are in a hurry, to send him packing. All we risk in return is that look that says, "What did I do wrong? Forgive me! I love you." Do we deserve all this love? Of course not. We fall far short of it. And the realization that we don't live up to that love is frustrating, disturbing and unforgettable. You insisted that I tell you about my animals; I couldn't do it without mentioning Sunday. But it's not the right time for me to be telling you this while you are grieving Julian, it's insensitive of me. The death of an animal is not the death of a brother. It's on an entirely different scale.

A dog is happy, obedient and submissive when he is with his master. This is how we exercise our power over him, over all animals, without limit and without exception. Man has enslaved animals for hundreds of years, never questioning this domination. We're in the twenty-first century yet we're still eating them, hunting them, fishing them, training them, torturing them, beating them, butchering them, locking them up, exterminating them, I could go on . . . It makes me sick to my stomach. What right does man have to behave like this? We know the answer: the belief in his superior intelligence. But is it really intelligent to use and abuse the weakest? I have overwhelming compassion for animals, as you can see. It's gut wrenching, I howl with rage at the images and videos aired by animal rights activists (when I have the courage to watch) that expose our evil treatment of them. This morning, I learned that the Chinese buy 1.8 million donkey skins from Africa each year; an essential ingredient for their remedies. The poor animals are killed with hammers. God forbid! After learning about such horrors, I console myself by devoting my time to animal welfare. I could have chosen other causes. There are so many. If I didn't do something, I'd risk getting depressed and becoming misanthropic.

Hadrian wanted to move to the country. I agreed, on the condition that we took in animals rescued from the slaughterhouse. My two cows are Prim'Holsteins called Mezzo and Soprano. They are so sweet when they lay their heads on my shoulder. I got Chocolate, my donkey, from a shelter. He is rather unsociable. He's afraid of everything. I have been trying to reassure him he isn't in danger for three years, without any success. But he trusts Yamaha, my

horse. I bought Yamaha from a riding club that was going
to send him to the abattoir, as he was too old and weary.
I also have two pigs I rescued from a battery farm. I was
allowed to take them as they were ill. They spent the first
few days terrorized and squeezed up against the back of
their pen. They would bang against the back wall if I tried
to approach them. Later, they came out but were extremely wary. They would run and hide as soon as I moved or if
they saw something moving outside. For the first time, they
were able to feel the ground and the grass beneath their
hooves and walk freely, experiencing daylight, sunlight,
fresh air, trees, the horizon. And for the first time, they
rolled in the mud! When I watch an imprisoned, mistreated
animal discovering freedom (well, semi-freedom), I know
that all the effort is worth it. After nursing them back to
health, I introduced them to the village children. They were
afraid of the pigs but didn't dare say so. They had no idea
that pigs were so big. So they jokingly asked, "When are
you going to make ham from them, Jean?" or "Are they the
ones we make hot dogs with?" They came up with names,
all of which I flatly turned down, such as Fat and Lard, Ba-
con and Eggs, Sausage and Chipolata, and so on. But the
kids learned to respect them and eventually named them
Alfred and Robert. My animals live in two huge meadows.
On weekends, the children knock on my door to help me
feed them and muck out the pens. They talk to them and
stroke them. It's a victory, and a step in the right direction
in terms of their education. I managed to tame Alfred and
Robert. They have almost become affectionate. I wonder
if animals that are lucky enough to escape hell remember
their past or whether they forget it? I never got another dog
after Sunday. I couldn't go through that pain again. You
should read aloud this excerpt from *Dogs*, a remarkable
essay by the philosopher Mark Alizart:

To which I would add: this angel also—this angel above all—is a dog, one of those that run excitedly ahead of their master, constantly looking over their shoulder to make sure the walking catastrophe that we are is still following along behind. Thy master, a dog.

Jean is interrupted by the doorbell. It's Luc. He says he hasn't come to apologize but that he doesn't like the way things were left. Jean invites him to stay for dinner. They avoid touchy subjects. The evening ends with music, with her giving him the rare pleasure of her piano playing. She plays Chopin's *Nocturnes*, Gershwin's *Rhapsody in Blue* and Debussy's *Valse romantique*. Luc stands next to her watching her fingers on the keyboard, her body moving to the music, her face relaxed and smiling. He gets home late. He has never seen her like this. To play for such a long time, with no pain in her hands, has done Jean a world of good. She will finish her letter later.

I can picture you, Samuel, as if I were there. I can imagine what you're thinking: this old fuddy-duddy lives on seeds and earthworms, washes her hair with crushed avocado, lives by candlelight, and wears jute sacks for clothes. Aha! No, not at all. I'm not a fundamentalist. I don't eat meat, I have a compost heap, a water butt that collects rainwater, sustainable vineyards and I avoid plastic as much as I can. But I think that's it. (I have been trying hard to follow Esther's advice and not to overuse interjections, yet here I am doing it again!)

I'll end my letter with this quote from George Thorndike Angell, an American lawyer and animal rights advocate:

I am sometimes asked, "Why do you spend so much of your time and money talking about kindness to animals when there is so much cruelty to men?" I answer: "I am working at the roots."

Jean

Samuel to Jean

5th April

Hello Jean,

Ben has been my best friend since primary school. In secondary school, he was the skiver. Now it's the other way around. He got his BTEC and since then he's been working in a restaurant. He didn't continue his studies because he wanted to cook and earn money. His parents are struggling. But now he regrets it because he says he doesn't have the basic training he needs for this career. He's going to try to go to catering college. I'd love to be able to tell you that Ben is like a brother to me, but I would feel like a traitor towards Julian. We went to see that cabaret act at the Zèbre de Belleville venue and had a fab time. We would never have gone if we hadn't got free tickets. That place rocks; there are singers, dancers and storytellers. It's quite hardcore and a bit risqué, we had a great laugh. On the way out I heard some girl say it was "burlesque in all its splendour". I looked up what "burlesque" meant on my phone. She's right. I had to do the same with your interjections, I couldn't remember what they were.

Actually it's not true that I don't go to Paris any more. I still go for the occasional demo. I don't give a toss what the demo is about. I just like being in the crowd, jam packed in the middle of frenzied people who are hyped up and shouting. I love this kind of atmosphere. I've marched with Act Up, students in front of the Pantheon protesting against the rise in tuition fees for foreign students, I've marched against climate change, and for housing, illegal migrants, and hospitals. It makes me feel like I'm someone, you know, part of a community. At the beginning, I went there to pick up girls, but I quickly realized it wasn't the right place. They're always in groups, it's hard to get their attention. Well, it depends, there are some nice ones. But I feel like an idiot next to them. I'm attracted to student types who shout and chant loudly. When they are interested in me, I freak out as soon as they ask me anything. I'm no good at it and prefer to leave. I have friends who are ace at chatting up girls, but not me.

I don't think you're an old fuddy-duddy at all. And now that I've told you why I go to demos, you're going to think I'm a dickhead. My mum is an environmentalist like you, but it's Julian's illness that made her that way. She has a phobia of germs and toxic products. She makes her own cleaning products. She analyzes the composition of everything she buys using that app Yuka. In fact no one goes out the door without Yuka's permission now. Have you heard about this app? We eat meat once a week from the butcher. I don't know if I told you that my mother is a prison nurse. It's tough, but she likes her job because she feels useful to the prisoners and the guards. What she hates and says she'll never get used to is the smell inside which is musty, damp, wet, scared, angry and vengeful. I like the way she describes it. She put an essential oil diffuser in our living room to help her "forget the smell of prison faster". Since our flat is small, you can smell it everywhere, but I'm used to it now.

I like what you wrote about animals. I personally believe that one day there won't be a single animal left on earth. No more elephants, lions, grasshoppers, deer, flies, butterflies . . . They'll be extinct. Humans will still be there. We'll have found other stuff to eat. Those who remember the last animals on earth will miss them, and their children won't understand why as they won't have seen any. They'll think, animals are naff, something out of Noah's Ark. Clones are the same, just better.

I haven't started *For Whom the Bell Tolls*.

Samuel

John to Nicolas

Tunis, 12th April 2019

Nicolas,

This is me, take it or leave it: I had a talent for business, got rich quick and my favourite hobbies were buying expensive cars, and collecting watches and Hermès suits. I never doubted or questioned anything for twenty-five years, never thought about what meaning I was giving to my life. I fired hundreds of people without an iota of guilt. I had targets to meet. Then a strange thing happened. Just before my fiftieth birthday, I sold my watches then my cars. Not to make money, but they were just getting in the way and cluttering up the place. I was tired of accumulating possessions. Sick of it. The more I got rid of, the lighter and happier I felt. I just wanted to have a clear out. I don't really know why I felt so euphoric afterwards, which if anything, was worrying. "What now?" I asked myself once everything was sold. Nothing . . . I was like a deflated balloon. I had created a vacuum by offloading all the trappings of my wealthy existence, and once everything was gone I asked myself: what do I do with the rest of my life?

If Boris needs me one day, I hope I won't let him down. In any case, thank you for telling me about your father. You're right, I do sometimes react strangely. I mean, it's hard to tell my kids how I feel. The next day I wondered if Emma thought I was a complete loser.

The weather in Chicago was dreadful. My conferences went well, but I couldn't free up any time for the museum. I haven't told my daughter I'm doing a writing workshop. It didn't occur to me. I'm not sure I want her to know.

John

P.S. I can't wait to try your *je ne sais quoi*—I love sea urchins.

Nicolas to John

Paris, 20th April 2019
(Dialogue)

Hello John,

I don't know if you realize what an alarming picture you're painting of yourself. I know a few guys like you, they represent everything I loathe. They flaunt their money, enjoy their company's dividends and don't give a damn about the poor people they fire. Yet despite this, I quite like you. I'm not convinced you really are that kind of person, deep down. You're too upfront, and you question yourself. And you know what? You should take my grand theories and judgments with a pinch of salt, because my prices are not exactly the cheapest. In fact, I am fighting a permanent tug of war with my conscience. In my defence, I calculate my prices as accurately as possible. Once I've paid my staff, my suppliers and my rent, I'm comfortable, but not wealthy by any means. This is an example of a frequent conversation I have with my guilty conscience:

"Hey Nicolas, aren't you getting a little carried away with your sixty euro starter?"

"But there's sea urchin in it, and they cost a fortune."

"There's ONE sea urchin in it!"

"Yes, but with caviar . . ."

"Come off it, you can literally count the eggs."

"I don't have a choice. At fifty-five euros, there's no profit margin. Besides, it's really delicious . . ."

"Do I have to remind you how much you used to charge for your traditional ham and pasta shells recipe, 'reimagined' with a white truffle sauce? It was the price you 'reimagined' more like . . ."

"Shut up, you're pissing me off."

"If your father saw that . . . By the way, since you're so sure of yourself, why don't you invite him over one of these days and show him the menu with your new ramped up prices?"

"There's no better value for money in Paris than my lunch menu."

"That's true, but who benefits from it? Businessmen. Do you remember that restaurant project you had, working with the mentally disabled?"

"As soon as I've got time, I'll start working on it, promise."

"Yeah, sure you will."

See you later, alligator.
Nicolas

CONVERSATIONS

Jean to Juliette

Verjus-sur-Saône, 6th April 2019

Hello Juliette,

Here is my dialogue.

So, it took the birth of your child for your own birth to boomerang back and hit you in the face. You could have had a normal pregnancy and birth, as if nothing was amiss, continuing to deny your past. That would have been surprising and worrying for both of you, don't you think? In your postpartum depression, I see a mirror effect between two mothers: your own and the new mother you've become. And between two daughters: Adele and yourself. You broke that mirror for Adele. I'm not a therapist, it's just a feeling—my hunch, you could say.

I like the sound of Nicolas from what you've written. When I see my neighbours come back from the supermarket, their car boots crammed full of junk food, it infuriates me. It's good to get indignant! Think about it. In the village, we have a particularly good bakery, run by a nice young couple. However, many of the locals prefer to buy industrially processed bread from the supermarket. One day, I saw my neighbour, Natalie, unpacking her groceries, so I came out of my house and offered to lend her a hand. Any excuse to talk about baguettes. As she was in a hurry and had bought

enough provisions to see her through World War Three, she
accepted. As I took the vacuum-packed steaks and chicken
nuggets out of the car, I gritted my teeth. She had made an
effort with the eggs, so that's where I began.

"I don't know these eggs, Natalie. Free-range, organic. You
must tell me what they are like."

"Oh yeah," she replied. "You have to be careful with
eggs. I've seen pictures of battery hens, it's disgusting. You
know that world inside out, Jean; I'm not going to teach
you anything new. The supermarket was heaving with people, it was a nightmare, hardly any parking spaces either."

"Those paper napkins are pretty."

"Yes, they have some really nice ones, I have to stop myself
buying them all up."

"Is this bread good?"

"It's okay, it's bread."

"Ah. Did you know that the bread in the village is excellent? If you want, I can bring you some back when I go there
in the morning."

"Thanks, but I buy up several loaves at a time and freeze
them for the week."

"I'll give you a piece to try and you can compare. Besides
it's those young people's livelihoods at stake. What if the
bakery goes out of business?"

"That's true; each time I tell myself I'll drop by there on
the way home. The trouble is I don't pass through the village
and am afraid of forgetting, so it's quicker for me to get it
at the supermarket . . . Stop looking at my ham like that!
Since you took Sacha to see your pigs, he refuses to eat it.
You should be glad; I'm not buying as much. I give him beef
steaks instead."

"I'll have to show him my cows . . ."

"Stop it, Jean, he needs calcium. You're going to turn
my son into some veggie or vegan I don't know what.

Come on, we're not going to start eating insects and seeds now are we?"

"Insects could be extinct in a hundred years' time anyway," I grumbled.

Brimming with frustration and despair, I walked off into my meadows to seek solace with my four-legged friends.

Jean

P.S. I think you write well, Juliette. I hadn't noticed your lack of coordinating conjunctions. Esther spots our mistakes a mile off and a good thing, too!

Juliette to Jean

Malakoff, 19th April 2019

Jean,

My dialogue is in this letter.

Esther's dialogues are a blessing. I laughed as I read yours. I'm delighted to hear that you are defending your village bakery. The sad thing is, the French are eating less and less bread. Bread bashing has been popular for a while now, on the pretext that too many bakers sell bad bread, it makes you fat, not to mention the gluten intolerance that half the population seem to suffer from. Do the French really have such bad taste that they prefer to buy that industrial stuff from supermarkets that tastes and feels like cardboard? Us bakers have had to turn to wholemeal bread. Women watching their weight swear by it. It's true that it's nourishing, keeps longer and supposedly stimulates your digestion. However (for your eyes only), it doesn't taste as good as farmhouse bread or traditional loaves!

You didn't tell me that you kept pigs and cows. Are you vegan? I eat very little meat, but lots of fish and eggs. Normal, you might say, for a fishmonger's daughter. Nicolas and I are making progress. I asked him why he behaved so badly when I got out of hospital. He said he didn't know what to make of me any more and was afraid of my reactions. He was exhausted; if he could have, he would have gone away for a while, leaving me alone with Adele. Hearing this saddened me. It stuck in my throat. But putting myself in his shoes, I suppose I would have reacted the same way. Writing is doing me a world of good. It forces me to think before replying. If, instead of writing it, he'd said all this to my face, I would have panicked, twisted his words, thought he no longer loved me and suggested we go our own separate ways.

Last night I dreamed about my parents. I woke up in a state, crying. I was suffocating, like in the worst days of my depression. I haven't seen them since I gave birth, when Adele was one day old. It was very painful to see them; they fawned over their granddaughter while I was in shock from what was happening to me and feeling totally disconnected from my daughter. They reminded me of my birth and my adoption. Their presence was hurting me, unwittingly. I didn't know what was happening any more. I just wanted them to go. I'm not ready to write to them yet.

Before the workshop, it would never have occurred to me to write them a letter. But what better way to explain what happened to me? I'm so fragile that I have trouble finding the words and keeping my emotions in check. I want them to know just how much I love them and how grateful I am to them.

My parents owned a fishmonger's shop in Trouville. They worked hard. In the winter when the outside temperature is below zero it's no fun having your hands in ice at six o'clock in the morning. I would say to them: "I'm Juliette, the hottest radiator on earth", and they would drop everything—knives, fish, crates etc.—and I would take their frozen hands between mine and blow hot air on them to warm them up. They would laugh and say: "Oh, that's better, our hands are all warm now." They happily played along with me, pretending to be amazed, as if me blowing hot air on their hands was magical. Not once did they push me away and say: "Wait a minute, it's busy" or "Later darling, we're in a hurry". The customers had to wait. After school, I would sit in the back of the shop to read and do my homework. My father and I went boating on Sunday afternoons. We didn't fish, we just sailed to see the sea and chat.

"You see, my Juju," he said, "the horizon is yours for the taking. Your mother and I are here to offer you the horizon and a good future."

"What's a good future?"

"It's for when you grow up. It means having a job and a home that you like."

"Do you have a good future?"

"My future is wonderful because you and your mother are in it. Before you came along, the horizon wasn't as bright . . . It's nice here, isn't it?"

"Yes. What kind of job will I have?"

"The one you want. You've got time to decide."

"The one I want?"

"Yes."

"A schoolteacher?"

"Yes, why not?"

" Fishmonger?"

"Yes, could do."

"Vet?"

"Yes."

"Astronaut?"

"Yes. But watch out, it's not going to fall out of the sky into your lap. To succeed you have to get your arse into gear. Don't tell your mother what I just said!"

Our conversation always ended like this. I would call out a list of jobs and at the end he always said: "You have to get your arse into gear though," which made me howl with laughter. I do miss my parents.

With best wishes,
Juliette

P.S. Sorry for replying late yet again. I had no idea what to write for the dialogue, when suddenly . . . eureka!

Jean to Samuel

Verjus-sur-Saône, 10th April 2019

Dear Samuel,

(This letter contains my dialogue).

Your mother must be a fine person. I wouldn't know how to cope with despair, anger, and probably violence too, on a daily basis like she does. I'm brave when it comes to animals, but not with humans.

Yes, I know the Yuka app. It's very useful, but I often forget to use it.

I don't see why you shouldn't have the right to think and say that Ben is like your brother. He was, I suppose, before Julian died. Has anything changed between you and Ben since then? And no, you are not betraying Julian.

I hope you watch out for yourself at demonstrations. I abhor the idiots who only go there to smash things up. I wouldn't like to think you protested against gay marriage or giving more individuals the right to IVF. This doesn't seem to be the case though.

Yesterday, I went for a walk with Sacha, my young neighbour. He is ten years old. His parents are nice, but unfortunately aren't the brightest of people. He is very intelligent though. Let's hope that nothing will spoil this child. I've written out our conversation for you:

"Hey Jean, did you know that I stopped eating ham?"

"Yes, your mother told me. She's not very happy about it either. Apparently, it's since you made friends with Alfred and Robert."

"Yeah, that's true. Can you imagine me eating them?"

"No, of course not. What do you eat instead?"

"Nothing special."

"Oh, right. You don't eat more beef steaks to replace it?"

"I don't think so. Why, are you against them? Do you ever eat steak?"

It had rained in the night. I skirted the puddles, while he had fun jumping in them.

"Each to their own, Sasha, but no, I don't eat steak. Do you know what animal it comes from?"

"Yes, it's from a cow."

"Exactly."

I held back from taking him by the hand into the meadows to see my cows. I was already imagining the scenario: *Go on, stroke them, can you see that big gentle look in their eyes? And look . . . If I stand in the middle of them both . . . there you go . . . wait . . . look, you'll see, they put their heads on my shoulder.* He'd go home and tell his mother that he'd never eat meat again, and I could say goodbye to our walks forever.

"Do you know what I'm doing this afternoon with Mum?"

"No, tell me. Are your feet not wet?"

"No. I'm making the invitations for my birthday party. There's going to be eleven or twelve of us."

"That's true, it's next week!"

"Do you think I'll be able to stroke your donkey, Chocolate, one day?"

"I hope so. Would you like to?"

"Yeah, I would. He looks so sweet. Mum wants me to invite Brice. But I don't like him. He's not very nice. He goes to all the birthday parties only because the parents make us invite him."

"Is Brice the physically disabled boy?"

"Yeah, he is."

"It's good that he's invited. It can't be easy for him . . ."

"You sound like all the grown-ups. You have to invite him because he's disabled. He's not nice to anyone, he really isn't."

"Maybe he's jealous and sad that he can't walk and run like you lot."

"There you go again; all the grown-ups say the same thing."

I laughed. It was horrible, but I understood what he meant. With his scowling face, Brice didn't elicit much sympathy. It's hard to get a smile, a hello or a thank you out of him. I suddenly remembered, with shame, that I had offered to show him my animals last year, or the year before, but had never got round to it. I had forgotten him.

"Give him one last chance. Invite him over and let him play your games with your friends, the games he CAN join in. If you're not willing to do that, then frankly there's no point in him being there. I'm not taking his side, but I bet my bottom dollar that you don't generally pay him much attention and exclude him. Am I right?"

"He asks the parents to put video games on as soon as he gets there. Plus, he hates being disturbed."

"Well, pretend that the invitation is really from you then and not from your parents. He might feel differently then. I think it's worth a try."

We stopped at the bakery on the way home. I bought him a pain au chocolat and a baguette for his parents. We walked slowly. A hare darted across our path, then a second one. He didn't mention Brice any more, and didn't tell me what he thought of my suggestion. He was quiet and pensive.

"What do I have to do to get Chocolate to let me stroke him?"

This is precisely what I love about this child. His stubbornness, his honesty, and the lengths he is prepared to go to in order to achieve his goals.

"You have to be patient. That's all there is to it. You can talk to him, tell him anything you want. Even sing to him. And he'll slowly get used to you."

He kissed me goodbye in front of his house. "But that's still no reason for him to be like that—Brice, I mean."

Jean

Samuel to Jean

14th April

My dialogue is in this letter.

Hi Jean,

I don't know if I'm allowed to do this for my dialogue, but I've copied out a conversation between Ben, Lou and me about *Game of Thrones*. I couldn't think of anything else anyway. Lou is a friend of mine. She watches the show with her parents. I don't know if you'll understand what we're on about.

Samuel: LOL u c Reddit survey about battle MVP?

Ben: Share when u no result!

Samuel: Yessir

Samuel: Ok

Samuel: Both dragons AND Ghost are alive ICYMI

Ben: Yeah? Wot a crap episode IMHO

Lou: ???

Lou: Ghost ok but Jon's dragon?

Lou: Forgot his name

Lou: Vyserion?

Lou: Thought he wos dead

Ben: Rhaegar

Ben: No both still alive

Lou: Yeah strange tho

Lou: Lucky 4 him

I started *For Whom the Bell Tolls*. It's not easy, but I'm persevering. It's not like I have a choice. If I hadn't decided to read all my brother's books, I would have dropped this one. I get confused between the communists, the republicans, the phalangists, the fascists, the brigades, POUM, but it's okay, I look things up on the internet. There are some tough scenes in this novel, which you don't want to hear about. Those parts are unbearable; that's the word I was looking for. I didn't know it was possible to do this with a book. Though it's normal for a film. The massacre of the fascists in Pablo's village is horrific. Do you remember that bit? They are locked up in the town hall and come out, one after the other. The peasants are waiting for them, with pitchforks and rods and form a wall right to the foot of the cliff where the prisoners have to throw themselves off. Down below is the river. As time goes on, the peasants get more and more drunk. It gets worse and turns into a bloodbath complete with insults, mockery, and so on . . .

My parents don't know that I read. I lock myself in my room. I don't want them to see me. I don't know what they'd think if they knew I read Julian's books. They might think I was trying to copy him. It would piss me off if they thought something like that.

Samuel

Nicolas to Juliette

Paris, 11th April 2019

My dear Juliette,

You're getting better! Don't say "yes, but . . ." Don't quibble. It's obvious. You're having laughing fits with your daughter and a praline brioche has inspired you to invent a new cake (though I'm not sure how). I can just imagine you checking out the competition; dissecting their brioche, smelling it, chewing it, rolling bits of it between your tongue and your palate, mulling it over. I used to think you were so strong, rock solid, impervious to any form of the blues. How wrong I was. I'll never again look at you and think I'd like to be as strong and as cheerful as you. You're not that strong. You're not that cheerful. In other words, there's more to you than that. I like this new-found vulnerability of yours, but it's nothing new; it's always been inside you.

My tribute to blandness will be blue lobster, with almonds, grilled artichokes and candied yuzu peel. The dish will take the form of a water drop, made with egg whites. I want the diner to experience a crescendo of flavours so the yuzu and its powerful citrus fragrance will be in the centre of the drop, to be savoured in the very last mouthful. I'll add these lines from Lao Tzu to the menu: *Both salty and sour comprise everything we love. But in the middle lies the supreme flavour—which never fades.*

I like your plans for the mill. You've already worked with Alex and Joel, so not much chance of you guys falling out. When you've got the paperwork together, don't hesitate to call Armand. He'll tell you whether the business is viable.

I went to Bourg with Adele, for my father's birthday. I wish you could have seen the pair of them together. What a spectacle! I said: "You know, Dad, this is the first time that Adele has been so cuddly with someone; she won't leave your side." I could see that he was flattered by my remark but he wouldn't admit it in a month of Sundays. My father reminds me of a bear. A proud man. Big and kind. He shrugged and grumbled, "I'm not just anyone, I'm her grandad." I suspect it was love at first sight. Something was going on that my mother and I were oblivious to. I was rather envious. I could see both amazement and happiness on my father's face. If I had told you this story instead of writing it down, you would have said I was exaggerating. I swear I'm not. Sat on his lap, facing him, Adele touched his eyebrows, his nose, his cheeks, his mouth, and gave him massive smiles. Then she pulled herself up and put her head on his shoulder and just stayed there. It was a beautiful moment.

My mother couldn't believe her eyes. She has been taking care of her granddaughter all day every day for the past three months and has never yet received such a display of affection from her. It amused her in fact:

"That's rich!"

"Your daughter has figured it all out already," said my father to me with glee.

"What do you mean by that?"

"Do you remember what I was like with you when you were little?"

"Err, no?"

"I didn't let you and your sister get away with anything. You had to toe the line."

"Yes, I know."

"Well, your daughter, I'm telling you, will be able to get away with anything she likes, whether you and Juliette approve or not. That's what grandparents are for, to spoil their grandkids."

I wish you could have been there, and I wondered what you would have said to him. Me and Adele can't wait for you to come home. Time is dragging by.

N.

P.S. In your dreams I no longer want to suddenly vanish when you're naked in front of me. It's unthinkable!

Juliette to Nicolas

Malakoff, 15th April 2019

Nicolas,

If I had to go back to the source of my breakdown and describe it in a few words, this is what I would write: When I saw Adele and took her in my arms for the very first time, I was overwhelmed by one obsessive question. *How could my mother have abandoned me?*

My whole life, I have wondered why she gave me up. Curiosity, nothing more. I thought of my birth mother as a separate entity, almost as if she had nothing to do with me. I didn't think, "Why did <u>my mother</u> abandon me?" but "Why did <u>this woman</u> abandon me?" This stranger. I couldn't understand. It took the birth of Adele for me to ask myself how it was possible. This woman who gave birth to me became an obstacle between me and my child. She carried me for nine months, heard my first cry, maybe also looked at me, held me in her arms, and kissed me. So yes, how could she abandon me? And leave me nothing?

Now she no longer comes between Adele and me.

I'm healing.

Last week, the doctor suggested that I take Adele to the park near our flat instead of the maternity unit. He felt that I didn't need their support any more and that it was time for the final assessment. As the weather was nice the day before yesterday, I did as he suggested. I didn't say anything to your mother. I was uptight. I'm used to being around mothers who have had postpartum depression and who are—how can I put it?—probably more worried, less spontaneous, and defensive with their child. It went well, even though I didn't feel as comfortable with Adele as the other mums were with their children. For them, everything seems natural, innate. Adele and I got to know each other ten months later than they got to know their babies. I take responsibility for this (I have to) and try to convince myself that this gap where I was absent won't damage our future relationship. When she looks at me and smiles, we are one. I can see in her eyes that she forgives me and loves me. Sometimes waves of tenderness wash over me and flood me with happiness; it's becoming a regular occurrence. Are you pleased to hear all this, my sweet?

With much love and affection,
Juliette

P.S. I'm sure your blandness theme will be a hit but be careful not to overthink your dishes.

John to Esther

Paris, 16th April 2019

Hello Esther,

Conversation in the Tuileries gardens.

Last Sunday, in a moment of madness, I went up to the man with the dachshund. I sat waiting for him on the bench where he usually takes a break, near the Jeu de Paume museum. I saw him coming from afar. He sat down next to me. From my balcony, he looked younger, thinner, and livelier. He must be in his seventies.

"Hello. Sorry to bother you, but are you the man with the dog I see from my balcony every morning around seven o'clock? I live up there, on the fifth floor, the windows with the wine-coloured curtains."

"It's most probably me, unless someone else walks their dachshund at that time. It's possible, they're quite a popular breed you know."

I then realized that he sported the same beige overcoat in summer and winter. Sitting a few inches away from him, I couldn't help but notice the worn sleeves, and how grubby his coat looked. My first reaction was how stupid I was talking to a tramp and even pointing out to him where I live. As he walked in the Tuileries gardens every day it hadn't occurred to me that he might be in need.

"What is his name?"

"She's a girl. Belinda."

"How old is she?"

"Eight. Do you have a dog?"

"No, I don't. I like them, but I'm not home very often. I travel a lot, so it would be impossible to deal with."

"You are lucky to travel around like that. I know France like the back of my hand, but overseas is a different story. My wife and I might go to the Canaries next summer."

"Do you live in the area?"

"Yes, in rue de Castiglione."

· He gave me an amused look but didn't say anything else.

I was reassured. "So, we're neighbours."

"Yes, you're right, we are neighbours. But I live up on the seventh floor under the eaves, with my wife and my dog, in a two-room studio."

I just sat there, struck dumb. Typical. The first time I try to engage in conversation with a stranger, I choose some poor sod who's skint.

"I didn't mean to embarrass you," he said. "Don't pull that face, it's not your fault. But you said 'neighbours', as if we moved in the same circles and you seemed relieved. We've got all we need in those two rooms. We're used to it. And then there's the Tuileries gardens for Belinda. They're a stuck-up bunch in this neighbourhood, to be honest, but we don't pay attention to it any more."

I smiled.

"Why do you watch people like that from your balcony?" he went on. "Having said that, I guess the view must be rather unique, is it not? We can see a small piece of the sky from our rooms, which is better than nothing."

"It's soothing. In a way, it's like I'm walking with them. Are you retired?"

"You could say that. I don't work any more, but what I get is peanuts. What about you, what do you do?"

"Business."

"Business? That's a funny word. I've noticed that there are two types of people who say they do 'business'. Those who don't like what they do and don't want to elaborate, or crooks. Well? Which are you?"

I smiled, again. I liked him.

"Good point. I'm not a crook. What did you do before you retired?"

"I was a professional clown. And I was funny."

"A clown? That is funny!"

"Yes, I was a funny clown."

I burst out laughing.

"I started young. I loved entertaining the littluns. I wanted to be a clown ever since I was a kid. Even today with this lousy pension, I don't regret it. I was the prankster, the Auguste clown, the one with the red nose. I wore the big clodhoppers and the checked dungarees, you get the picture? With Pierrot, the white face clown, we did the classic slapstick show—you know, the water fights, face slapping, trumpeting, you name it. We had one accident after another; I was the king of blunders. I would knock my friend to the ground without meaning to. I carried a rake on my shoulder and would turn around suddenly and bang! he would get it in the face. Or when I tried to fix the garden hose, he would get drenched from head to toe, but I didn't realize as I was busy concentrating on repairing it . . . In short, all the gags that make generations of children howl with laughter."

"Did you retire long ago?"

"I was sixty-one years old. My wife got ill. I stopped working to take care of her. She's better now. Anyway, I was fed up with it, I was weary. When I met her, I was fifty. She's not a circus girl. She was a cleaner here, in this area. For years, she's been working for an Italian lady who is away a lot and who befriended her and lets us stay in her maid's rooms. We've been there for nine years now. My wife continues to clean for her and we prepare the flat if Mrs Ada or someone from her family comes to Paris, and I drop by every night to check that all is okay. It reassures her. Are you married? Do you have children?"

"I'm divorced and my children are grown up."

"Oh, well you shouldn't stay single, it's not good for your morale! I enjoyed talking with you, Mr. Businessman, but I must go now, otherwise I know someone who'll worry."

"It was nice to get to know you. I hope we will meet again."

We smiled at each other but didn't shake hands. He radiated kindness. I watched him leave, with his dog on a leash. I realized I hadn't asked him his name, but it was too late. I had made the acquaintance of a clown who lived in rue Castiglione.

Did you like my story, Esther? Fiction or reality in your opinion?

John

Esther to John

Lille, 20th April 2019

Hello John,
    Mother–daughter (non) dialogue.

I fell for your clown story right until the last sentence. You have a real talent for storytelling. Fiction or reality? You tell me.

This morning at breakfast, the atmosphere with my daughter was—how can I put it?—charged. She has exams this week, hasn't revised and is taking it out on me. Don't worry I'm used to it. Since I owe you a dialogue, this is my chance to inflict our painful conversation on you.

"Hi, Mum."

"How are you, sweetheart, did you sleep well? Do you want some grapefruit juice?"

"I had nightmares, I dreamt about my exams, it was horrible. White grapefruit is definitely better than pink."

"If you revised a bit, Pia, you'd sleep better, wouldn't you? Your nightmares at least prove that you're not totally oblivious to it all. I can never find white grapefruit juice, even in the supermarket next to the bakery. Here, have some toast."

"What, you think it's normal that I have nightmares?! No thanks, it's burnt."

"Of course not. I think it's normal for you to revise, which isn't the same thing. You'll do well, I'm sure. You can have my toast, it's just as you like."

"No, there's black bits on it too. I'll make some more. I'll ask Nina where her mum buys white grapefruit juice."

"Speaking of black bits, you didn't skimp on the mascara this morning . . ."

"Mum, stop it! I dreamed that in maths I wasn't given the same exam paper as the others and spent the whole hour wondering why. I handed in a blank page to Mrs Gervais, who said, 'Well, it won't take long to correct yours!' The butter smells weird, don't you think? Here, take a whiff."

"Smells all right to me."

"I'm telling you it smells weird."

"How does it smell to you?"

"Rancid."

"I only bought it last week. The expiry date is 10th May. That's ages away."

"Yes, but sometimes they get it wrong. As you can see!"

"I was thinking that it would be nice to go to Croatia this summer. Mathilde did it last year, she really liked it. She rented a small house on an island just off Split and—"

"If you insist, but I'd rather go somewhere you can get to by train. For the planet, you should only fly once a year max, and we've already flown this year. It's simple. A passenger flying just over half a mile produces 285 grams of CO_2, compared to only 14 grams by train, and it's the same for—"

"We'll see, Pia. I have to go. I'll let you clear up. Love you."

"Love you too."
Some mornings, I can't leave quickly enough.

Esther

P.S. If you ever meet my daughter, don't tell her that you fly roughly two hundred times a year. You never know, she might just poison your drink.

John to Nicolas

Paris, 24th April 2019

Hello Nicolas,
   (My dialogue is below)
   Thanks for that line, "guys like you represent everything I loathe". Clearly you and Esther both think I should be hung, drawn and quartered. Yet I've only ever shown compassion to you both. I'm rather astonished.
   I wonder where my guilty conscience went. It disappeared years ago.
   I had a slanging match with my mother yesterday, on the phone. A bit stupid at our age. She's over eighty; there should be a statute of limitations or something. To give you some context, here is a brief description of my parents. My mother is a capricious member of the upper bourgeoisie, and my father is spineless and lets her get away with murder. His favourite phrase is, "As you wish, my dear." She called me to tell me that they had put their house in Honfleur up for sale. It infuriated me to hear this. My mother loves to buy second homes, move into them and sell them a short while later. But she is impulsive. With her, everything is great at first, but then she gets bored and wants something

new. Her husband takes care of everything: the move, the
paperwork, the appointments with the solicitor and the estate agent, and so on. The Honfleur house was practical,
and all on one level with friendly neighbours nearby. I had
hoped it would be their last move. It was perfect for my
father, who likes the countryside and has difficulty getting
up and down stairs.

"I saw a flat in Nice—it looked lovely."

"Dad likes Honfleur, doesn't he?"

"Oh, you know your father, it doesn't matter to him where
he lives."

"But Mum, we're not talking about a pot plant. You know
he's very attached to this house."

"Your father is a big boy now, he doesn't need his son to
tell him what he wants. Especially since you've never even set
foot in that house."

"What's that got to do with it? I don't need to go there to
know that he's happy there. May I remind you that not so
long ago, you thought it was absolutely *faaabulous*. But he's
never stood up to you . . . And who's going to take care of the
move, the sale, the paperwork? Him, as usual! Do you ever
think about that?"

"Oh dear! You've been eating mad cow; I swear you have!
Do you have a problem, John? I'd like you to speak to me
with a little more respect, please. And—"

I started shouting down the phone in the lobby of JFK,
pacing back and forth at full speed. I shouldn't have mim-
icked her snobbish tone; it was mean of me. My hands were
sweaty. The security staff and other passengers were giving
me sidelong glances, but I didn't care.

"He'll get bored in Nice. He doesn't like it there. But you
don't care about that. Can't you, for once in your life, just
once, please him and stay in Honfleur? Is that asking too
much of you?"

"I know better than you what your father needs. And I would like—"

"You would like? Who cares for once what *you* would like! You're going to inflict yet another move on Dad. You must be out of your mind!"

My heart was pounding in my head. If I didn't calm down soon, I was going to have a heart attack. I had a crazy urge to lash out and tell her exactly what I thought of her. My body was raging and my head was about to explode.

"If you just let me finish my sentence . . . I would like you to speak to me nicely. I'm as old as your father, you know, and—"

"Do you know the stupidest thing I've ever done? Waiting all this time to tell you to stop behaving like a spoilt brat and—"

She had the good sense to hang up on me. I was going to tell her how stupid and vain she is.

John

Nicolas to John

Paris, 28th April 2019

Hi John,
  Parisian monologue.
  I have always talked to myself when I'm wearing my helmet. It's my way of releasing pent up stress. It's hard not to be a nervous wreck when you're riding a moped around this city. I'm always surprised when I make it to my destination in one piece. So let's take a spin around Paris!

Hey excuse me, WTF! You can't see me, you dumb ass, because your eyes are glued to your phone! You almost crushed me there with your has-been four-by-four. I'm out of here, before I smash your rear-view mirror and your ugly mug if you so much as dare to open your window and insult me. I remember when Fredo relocated to a suburb near Brussels. I gave him six months. Why the hell doesn't he move over on the right? But I was wrong. He's been there three years now. He's happy, calm and peaceful, surrounded by his trees and his bees. I don't believe it, he's stopped there? Jesus, what are all these new roadworks? Where am I supposed to go? Fredo is rather highly strung, but I understand what he meant now, when he said to me upon leaving: "I love this city, but I can't live here anymore. Too much action, it's stress overload, I can't channel my energy. I'm caught up in the whirlwind of it all." He's right, you have to be permanently on your guard. Your senses are bombarded from all directions. Holy shit, that geezer must be insane to put his kid on his scooter in the middle of all this traffic! Hey! Missus! She thinks she can do what she wants because she's a pedestrian? It's a good thing we're only going two miles per hour, otherwise she'd be in casualty by now. What a bitch . . . to top it all, she's having a go at him! And that dickhead acting the big man on his moped! It's not going to end well . . . Yeah, do you not think that I'm in a hurry too, idiot? What? They're drilling here too? That's absurd . . . I'm sure that jerk in front is on his phone as well . . . Wait until I catch up with you, you little—

Nicolas

WAITING

Nicolas to Juliette

Paris, 18th April 2019

Dearest Juliette,
　You ask if I'm pleased to hear that you're feeling better? The word "pleased" is rather an understatement to describe how I feel. To put it in a nutshell, I can now see light at the end of the tunnel. All I think about is your return. It's obsessing me. Yesterday, I went to see Aunt Marie. She was watching TV when I arrived. The nurse accompanied me to her new room, which is nicer than her old one. It's smaller but overlooks the park. Since Esther wants us to write a dialogue, this is a good opportunity to relate our nonsensical conversation to you:

　"Hello Auntie, how are you?"
　"Sit beside me, sir, and talk to me slowly. I didn't understand who you are."
　"I'm Nicolas, your nephew. Sylvie and Claude's son. Here, I've brought you some flowers and those cakes you like."
　"No, Nicolas is younger than you. At this time of day he must be in school."
　It was a bad start. I wanted to hug her and say, "You're right, I was nicer when I was younger. Who cares how old I

am?" She turned back to the television. It was some dumb quiz show I don't think she was following. I couldn't see anything in her eyes except emptiness. It was a nice day, so I suggested that we take a walk in the park. "Yes, all right," she answered in a dull voice. I took her coat from her wardrobe and fetched her Stan Smith trainers with Velcro fasteners. The nurse had warned me that she was adamant it had to be these shoes. She must have forgotten how to tie shoelaces. We walked past the reception desk, and she said to me:

"It's dreadful here. Luckily, I'm going home tonight."

"I don't think you're going home tonight, Auntie. Besides, it's not dreadful here."

"Stop calling me Auntie! I know what I'm saying."

She may have lost her memory, but not her bossy nature. When we were outside, she grabbed my arm.

"Mum sends her love," I said. "She'll come and see you on Wednesday."

She didn't answer.

"Is your room okay for you? Is there anything you need?"

Silence. "Sylvie brings me flowers."

I was happy that she could remember her sister's visits. My mother will be pleased when I tell her. She may have lost her marbles but physically, she's a firecracker. In the park, she was almost running.

"I brought you a bouquet too. All white, did you see? I know you love white flowers."

"Did you come by car? That's good, it means I can leave with you."

"Oh no, Auntie. I came on my moped, not in the car. Will you eat my chocolate cake later? And try my *financier* cakes?"

"Yes, I will. Who are you?"

"Nicolas, your nephew. Sylvie and Claude's son. From Bourg-en-Bresse."

"Yes, I know who you are, Nicolas."

She used my first name, so I think that's when she started to remember me a little.

"I had a daughter. Her name is Adele. She's eleven months old. Mum and I told you about her."

"Adele . . . that's rather old fashioned isn't it?"

"Err . . . do you think so?"

"Yes, I do. Don't you want to tell me what's going on in your life? I've had enough of people always asking me pointless questions like 'did you eat well?' and 'did you sleep well?' or 'do you have everything you need?'. No one ever tells me anything interesting any more."

I told her about the restaurant, my team, and the latest dishes I put on the menu. I reminded her that she dined there with her son when we had just opened, and that her sister was living in Paris with us to take care of her granddaughter, and that it's not easy to live with your mother again when you're in your forties. Plus I told her what you and I are going through . . . I got the impression that she was listening to me. There was a small glimmer in her eyes. I didn't imagine it. But when I was done, she said, "That's all dandy then."

We sat down on a bench in silence. Once back in her room, I spoon fed her some cake. There I was, feeding my aunt, the lady whom I was in awe of when I was a kid, her rigour, her demanding nature. She was the brainy one of the family, a university professor, a historian specializing in religious studies. I had to grit my teeth to stop myself from crying.

I put on my jacket. I was afraid she would want to go back with me, but she had forgotten. I kissed her goodbye. When I left, she didn't turn around, she was staring out of the window. My head was all over the place.

N.

P.S. I didn't ask you who else you write to. Is it Esther?

Juliette to Nicolas

Malakoff, 25th April 2019

Dear Nicolas,

I had what in theory should be my last meeting with the doctors. I told them it felt like they were throwing us out. One of them got a bit peeved and assured me that Adele and I were fine now, and that my psychiatrist would continue to monitor me. He couldn't resist saying that at the maternity unit they treat and protect vulnerable mothers but have to be careful that the ward doesn't become a cocoon that patients come to rely on.

They kindly organized a leaving party for us. The girls gave Adele some toys (you must have seen them, a teddy bear and some blocks). I cried. The next day I had some Basque tarts and cakes delivered to them.

I'm sorry about Marie. Your mother told me about it the last time I was there. She said she was looking for a care home for her in Bourg-en-Bresse so that she can be nearer to her when she returns home. We could go and visit her with Adele, what do you think?

I'm supposed to write a dialogue but have zero inspiration. I need to talk to you properly, not play at being a writer. I managed to come up with something for my other correspondent. It's not Esther, it's Jean. Do you remember her? She's quite some lady. She was a piano teacher in Lyon. Now she lives alone in the country with her animals. She was so easy to talk to, that I ended up confiding in her. She's a kind person and has been a great help to me. I don't know if she was a good piano teacher, but she would have made a fantastic therapist. I invited her to dine at Camellia (she doesn't eat meat) when the workshop is over. You'll like her. I'm thinking of a cake that I can name after her. That's how fond I am of her! Before I get home, I'll probably face a few tough sessions with my therapist. It's a long, slow process. I'll be totally drained afterwards. I don't want my low moods to affect you more than they should. I feel like I'm able to pick up the pieces and make sense of things now. Please wait for me and stand guard at the end of the tunnel. That's all I ask of you, my brave soldier.

With much love and affection,
Juliette

Jean to Samuel

Verjus-sur-Saône, 18th April 2019

Hello Samuel,
   A depressing and self-indulgent little monologue.

Why should I get out of bed? For whom? I've got no one waiting for me. Nothing to look forward to, zero prospects . . . How did I get to this point? Alone in a house in the country with my animals. I'm pathetic. I don't even have the piano to console me any more. Just my wailing. I should get up. Drink a coffee. What will be will be. What if I do some baking? Cakes galore. Here we go, radio on full blast. I don't want to hear the doorbell if it rings. Bam! Pow! Clack! Boom! Bang! I love making lots of noise, slamming the cupboard doors and rushing around, as if I were in a hurry. I must pay attention to the cooking time. My head is clearing, that's it, I'm breathing better. 1:00 pm already! My last cake is in the oven. Is that me, there, in the mirror? That mad woman with chocolate cake mixture on

her face, sugar in her hair, sticky fingers, and red cheeks?
I've made a crème caramel, an apple pie, a pear charlotte
and a chocolate mousse. I'm not expecting anyone, I've no
idea who'll eat them, but I feel better. Oh, this kitchen! It's
a minefield. I'm crazy, fit to be locked up. All this because
I got out of bed on the right side this morning.

I didn't understand your dialogue with your friends at all.
But it was a good idea.
    I remember only too well the scene you mention from
Hemingway's novel. You found the right word, "unbearable".
What a great book though, isn't it?
    I look forward to reading your monologue . . .CUL8R,
Jean

Samuel to Jean

23rd April

My monologue: In my brother's head.

This is Julian. I didn't talk about my death. I didn't say I
was afraid. This doesn't mean that I didn't think about it.
When I was in too much pain, I would shout 'get lost!' to
Sam. I didn't watch TV series, I avoided going out and
thinking about girls. When I was in pain, or afraid, I became aggressive. I hated my body, which had betrayed me
and given up on me a long time ago. Sometimes I hated
my parents, for turning me into such a wreck. Although
I tried not to show them. Deep down I knew it wasn't
their fault and that they would have sacrificed everything
for me. Sometimes I hated my brother too. He wasn't ill
but he moped around and did sod all work at school. I

could be funny. I was good at imitating people, especially the hospital staff. I had lots of opportunities to practise because I was always surrounded by doctors, nurses and orderlies, some of whom I had known for years. The one I imitated best was Florine, because she had a lisp. When we were kids, it made us laugh. She was the nicest person. And then Doctor John, with his various twitches and tics. When I came home, I was happy. Each time, I hoped that I was cured, that nothing would happen to me again. If the pain came back, or if I was too tired, I was the one who would ask to go back into hospital. My place was no longer with them. My mum couldn't look after me as well as the nurses, and I prevented her from going to work. As for my dad, he panicked as soon as I puked or had a fever. When things went downhill, I would drag my feet, hesitating to leave, thinking to myself that the people I loved the most in the world were powerless to help me and were unable to protect me. And that was an excruciatingly painful realization, even if it was the truth. It made me feel even more alone. Home and the hospital were two different worlds. Like day and night. I asked myself, 'Why me?' There was no answer, which depressed me. I may have been a wreck, I may have been in pain, but I was raging, like a bull. I liked uni. Soon I would be going back, I told myself. I wouldn't catch up, but it didn't matter any more. You can go to uni at any age, it's not like secondary school. I would study literature, maybe write books or go on to be a university professor. That's what kept me going, the future I imagined for myself, where I had my own role to play. Just like everyone else.

I didn't say goodbye to my parents or Samuel. I didn't know I was going to die. End of monologue.

Anyway, I need to tell you about the guidance counsellor. To calm my anxiety, I told myself that I didn't care, it would be over quickly, and that I was only going to please my dad. It didn't work out that way though. I was super stressed out. I had nothing to say to that woman. It must be like that when you take an exam and haven't revised. Besides, I didn't want to set foot in a school again. It wasn't the one I used to go to luckily; I would have refused outright. I didn't much like Mrs Dablon when I saw her. She's everything I don't like, skinny and wizened, with really short hair and piercing eyes. Which didn't help. She told me she was there to guide me, help me to see my future more clearly, and answer any questions I had. All I wanted to know was how long it would last, but I held back. I wanted to stay on her good side for my dad's sake. At first, we talked about anything and everything, what I do during the day, my favourite TV series. She likes *Peaky Blinders* and *Narcos* too. I was surprised she talked to me about them. She could tell that I was ill at ease and was trying to be nice. She was amused by the writing workshop. I don't see what's so funny about it. To me, it's serious. I told her that it's not easy to write, but that I am starting to enjoy it. I told her about you and that I'd started reading. She wanted to know what kind of books I read and whether I wanted to continue when the workshop was over. I told her that I did, and that there was no connection between the two. I didn't tell her about my brother's books. An hour later, I was still in her office. I couldn't take it any more. I wondered where she was heading with all her questions. That's when she offered to see me again. "We will discuss your future, and possible directions. In the meantime, think about everything you would like to do in life. What you would like to study, what jobs, what sports . . . anything you can think of. Write it all down on a piece of paper. I'll think about it too."

But I tell *you* everything that's on my mind. I'll just have to hand her a blank sheet of paper.

I didn't think there would be a second meeting. What a pain.

The more I read *For Whom the Bell Tolls*, the more I like it. Even the love story.

Samuel

Margaux cleans the house on Saturdays. She starts with Julian's room. She could just vacuum it occasionally but can't bring herself to neglect it in this way. She leaves the door ajar. She found out that Samuel has been going into his brother's room. She wonders what he does there. While dusting Julian's books, she notices that two of them are missing. She wonders if Sam has taken up reading. *That would surprise me, but it would be amazing. It would mean he's doing better, that he's interested in something.* She is relieved. A bit later, she finds a book by Eric Faye in his chest of drawers on top of his T-shirts. She thinks it best not to encourage or congratulate him or risk ruining everything. If he wanted her to know, he wouldn't have tried to hide it from her. She has already done enough damage. It's largely her fault that Sam is sullen, self-conscious and withdrawn. Julian's illness monopolized all her time and attention. Her youngest child had to fend for himself. All he got were the crumbs. Crumbs of her love, attention, time and support. Samuel had been pushed out. She and Patrick didn't bother with him enough. It wasn't fair on him. She knew it but couldn't do anything about it. Each time Julian had relapsed, they plunged back into his illness. Nothing else mattered except their battle with the cancer. *I treated Sam lousily* she thinks to herself despondently, remembering the times she had to cancel an outing, forgot to ask him how his exams went or didn't renew his basketball membership.

Since Julian died, she doesn't know how to close the gap between them and ask for his forgiveness. She now realizes just how wide the gulf between them is. She tells herself it's too late. She doesn't remember him ever complaining about their attitude or throwing a single temper tantrum. Not even once in all this time. Although a tantrum, anything, would have been preferable to this torrid silence which he has retreated into. When they reproach him for his apathy and inertia, he just looks at them, expressionless.

Margaux knows better than anyone how damaging guilt can be. There is no better place than a prison to study the various forms of guilt and the harm it causes. There is the guilt that slowly kills you, the guilt that eats away at you from the inside, and the guilt that drives you insane and feeds off violence and death. Her guilt is double-sided: she feels guilty about her dead son and guilty about the surviving son she neglected. She sighs. *Guilt smothers you and prevents you from moving on. It's paralysing me and distancing me from the person I love most in the world.*

John to Esther

Tunis–Paris, 26th April 2019

Hello Esther,
    Here is my monologue: Nicole, wife of a clown.

I just love this little bit of sky in the corner of my window! It makes me want to go out for a stroll and leave behind this poky room that smells of wet sponge. It's that same smell you get in some bistros. I've tried everything to get rid of it. I aired the room for days, lit scented candles, bought cedar wood, left the fan on for hours; but it always comes back. When I notice it and ask Max if he can smell it too, he closes his eyes, inhales deeply, and says he can't smell a thing. I didn't sleep well last night. It's not going to get any better this week either, as the neighbour is on nights. I heard him come in around 4:00 am. He made himself something to eat, put the radio on at low volume, took a shower at the end of the corridor . . . There is nothing I can do. In spite of telling myself to go back to sleep and concentrate on something else, I visualize what he's doing, as if I were there with him on the other side of the paper-thin wall. He takes off his shoes, goes to the kitchen area, runs the water, opens his cupboard, then his drawer, takes some cutlery out, pulls out his chair . . . It's driving me nuts. Why won't my brain obey me when I ask it to stop focusing on the neighbour and come back to me? When I wake up exhausted and grouchy on mornings like these, I grumble and moan about our two tiny rooms. I tell Max that I want to move out, that I can't do it any more. He asks me where we'd go. I have no answer. When I whine like this, he takes his time coming back from the park. What am I complaining about? It's not that bad here. The two rooms connect, the toilets and the communal shower are clean, we have a lift. And with no rent to pay, we can treat ourselves. We go to the cinema and at the weekend we visit the all-you-can-eat buffet at a good Chinese restaurant. Besides, Max is all I need to make me happy. When he's out, I sometimes take advantage of his absence to air his clown costume, the bow tie, the hat and the shoes. I put them on the bed. I love their flamboyant colours, and delight in running my hand over the green velvet trousers, the red cotton and felt jacket, and the hat, on which I sewed big sunflowers. If we had had children, Max would have done his clown act for them, and then for our grandchildren after that. I can hear the lift stopping on the fifth floor. It's them coming back.

John

John imagines Esther to be a small brunette, with a bob and a pointed severe face and glasses. Prettyish, but not a head turner. What does it matter anyway? This Esther is merely a figment of his imagination. He digs out the email containing the photos of the workshop members. Juliette fits Nicolas's description. A pretty woman with a square face, wild dark hair, black eyes and thick eyebrows. Esther Urbain doesn't feature in the set of photos. When she asked the workshop members if they would prefer her feedback by phone or email, John chose email, for practical reasons. He regrets it now. At least he would have heard her voice on the phone. He searched on the internet, hoping to find a photo of her on her bookshop's website. He googled "Esther Urbain", "François Perceval and Esther Urbain", and then "Daughter of François Perceval". He found pictures of the writer, whose hair must have turned white prematurely, but nothing on his daughter. She's not on Facebook, Twitter or Instagram. She doesn't exist on social media. In some photos of François Perceval, you can see the same brunette appearing in the background each time, but nothing indicates that it's her. On social media there is only one Esther Urbain: a delightful child who explains "How to be yourself" in a YouTube video dated 2017.

Esther to John

Lille, 2nd May 2019

To John,
  "I love and hate": my easy monologue.

I love the snow. I hate umbrellas. I love red coats and jackets. I hate girls who wear too much makeup and dress to kill. I love *Bust of a Woman*, a sculpture of my mother that I have in my room. It's her watching over me. I hate folk music. I love Bach and Bowie. I hate queuing. I love dahlias, they remind me of my grandfather. I hate blue flowers and round bouquets. I love many writers. I hate the "it was better back then" customers, who only read the classics. I love chips with smelly cheese and pineapple. I hate endives with ham, and even more so the people who are surprised I hate them:

"How come? They're delicious when prepared right." I love my parents. I hate my parents. We shouldn't be allowed to die like that. I love people who love silence. I hate music in restaurants. I love kindness. I hate myself when I pretend not to see that homeless person on the pavement. I love those who doubt. I hate extremists of all stripes. I love looking through photo albums with photos of me with my parents. I hate it when melancholy comes knocking at my door when I didn't ask it to. I love Chopin and The National. I hate mawkish voices. I love being right. I hate cheapskates. I love the brave. I hate shirkers. I love westerns. I hate musicals. I love Jean Echenoz, I hate feel-good books. I love the artists Douanier Rousseau and Nicolas de Staël. I hate people in museums who photograph paintings without looking at them. I love the idea that one day I will tour Japan. I hate the smell of wet dog. I love the radio. I hate TV. I love myself when I make allowances for people. I hate people who eat with their mouths open. I love Edward Elgar and Benjamin Biolay. I hate love stories that end badly. I love fog. I hate cruise ships. I love bad weather.

Esther

John to Nicolas

Paris, 2nd May 2019

Hello Nicolas,

Here is my monologue: Inside my father's head. I heard her say, "Oh, you know your father, it doesn't matter to him where he lives", before she went to her room and closed the door behind her. At first I didn't understand who she was talking to, John or Pierre. She reappeared a few minutes later, absolutely livid.

"As if it's any of his business! After all I've done for him, that's how he repays me." When I asked her why she was so angry, she said, "It's John, he yelled at me. He doesn't understand why we're selling Honfleur as you love this house. What I want doesn't come into it, of course!" I said nothing. What's the point? I'll soon be dead anyway. What intrigues me though, is John's reaction. It's not like him. His mother's not going to change now, he's intelligent enough to know that.

If I could put the clock back fifty years, I would do things differently. I picture us, we're young, it's not long after we first met. We're in a restaurant. She's sitting opposite me. She makes a disparaging remark. One too many. I get up, slam my fist down on the table and holler, "That's enough! Don't ever talk to me like that again!" or even, "You're seriously pissing me off now!" I relish the look of shock and anger on her face. She holds my gaze and hesitates before answering, looking down at her plate. Of course, it didn't really happen like that. I gave in to her whims, and took her criticisms and accusations without defending myself. I was the fool not her. I thought how lucky I was that a woman like her was interested in a guy like me. She was stunning. And what class! Bright blue eyes, long blonde hair, a full mouth, a sweet voice, a slim waist . . . she was my ideal woman. I was hardly a ladies' man. At twenty-seven, I had a receding hairline, I was overweight, and I hated my podgy fingers. I was embarrassed about them and my yellow teeth. I smoked like a chimney, the strongest tobacco too. When that princess, the ultimate tease, frowned, and pouted, when she crossed her arms over her chest in anger, I laughed. I found it charming, idiot that I was. She showed herself as she was, tough and snobby, from our very first date. I wanted her for myself. I had the money to buy her. I wasn't worried about her bad temper. We would be happy together, and in time she would soften, even bloom.   I hadn't bargained on her despising me so quickly. Nor that I wouldn't be able to stand up to her. "She's gone too far this time, I must talk to her." "She can't speak to me like that in front of the children, it's unacceptable." I said those words to myself countless times. Days, months, years passed without anything changing. God knows why. During the first few years I was afraid of losing her, but after that? I must admit I was secretly glad that John cared about me enough to have a go at his mother. He's quite right, I would have preferred to stay in Honfleur.

John

Nicolas to John

Paris, 5th May 2019
My letter "ten years later".

Hi John,

On 15th February 2019, ten years ago to the day, I sent my first letter to a complete stranger. You. "This workshop is absurd, it's completely naff", is roughly what I was thinking at the time. I can admit this now. These forced exchanges reminded me of having to write to my German pen pal when I was fifteen. But I had no choice, you know that; I'm not going to repeat the story. I don't regret it. Juliette came back and I gained a friend. I was wondering how to celebrate the tenth anniversary of our friendship and our collaboration. Dinner at Camellia? Okay, but what else? Write to you, of course! This is my chance to tell you how glad

I am to have met you. I value our friendship. And without you, A Little Bit Different would never have seen the light of day. I had to push you, but we got there. I know myself. If you hadn't supported me, I wouldn't have gone through with it. A restaurant and two grocery stores, a real achievement, eh? We've got fifteen disabled guys working there now. Can you believe it? I get carried away by my enthusiasm, I've always been like this. Frankly, it's easier to cope with in writing. You and I have both seen how these young people have gained some independence, and how their work fulfils them. Naturally, you don't earn a dime working with me, but isn't this sort of success so much more meaningful than having loads of dosh?

Well, I've got to go and get back to the kitchen. I'm concocting a new dish with blandness as its theme: organic grasshoppers and ants, with garden grass and soya mousse. See you later, alligator,

Nicolas

Jean to Juliette

Verjus-sur-Saône, 29th April 2019

Juliette,

We spend our lives waiting for someone or something. I'm waiting for my daughter. Young Samuel is waiting for his parents to notice him. You're waiting until you feel ready to go home. I suppose Nicolas is waiting for you to come back. Esther could have asked us the question: What are you waiting for?

I enjoyed hearing your conversation with your father. Thanks for sharing.

There is something I must tell you. I have had a subscription to the Lyon Opera for years now. Last September, I hesitated before renewing it. I have to drive to get there, and Lyon is almost twenty miles from my house. I'm tired when I get back, and the subscription isn't cheap . . . One day when I was probably feeling on top form, I started to question my attitude. What was happening to me? Had I forgotten how to drive? Was I ill or tired? No, not at all. It then struck me that one of the first things old age does to us, is to trick us into giving up activities we enjoy. We become less motivated, more afraid, lazier; in short, we abdicate. It doesn't take much. We slowly but surely shrivel up and retreat into our shells and our world shrinks. The shift is barely noticeable, but it's real.

Struggling with old age is a daily battle, we can fight it if we've got our health. So I made a check list of all the little things I've given up without noticing until now. It was a real eye opener! I plan fewer dinners, I hardly ever go to the cinema, I don't know the latest classical and jazz artists, I change my sheets less and I use a shampoo that doesn't suit me (can't be bothered to buy the right one). Sorry for sharing such intimate details with you. I will continue my list. More to come, I'm sure. Do you realize that I almost gave up going to concerts, one of my most cherished pastimes?

This morning, I took a long walk with Luc, who runs the village bistro. I love his eccentric side and his generosity. He is currently trying to convince the mayor and the locals to welcome migrants to the village. His argument is that there are empty dwellings, shops have closed due to lack of custom and vineyard owners are struggling to find workers. Plus the elderly need assistance. I tell him to elaborate on his project, get it down on paper and put a figure on it. But he doesn't bother.

I hope that one day you will come and visit me. We'll go for a walk. When we have climbed to the top of my hill, I'll show you a viewpoint with no eyesores, housing estates or retail parks. Just vineyards, woods, forests, and empty space as far as the eye can see. I would be delighted to come to Paris and dine at Camellia.

Best regards,
Jean

Juliette to Jean

Malakoff, 6th May 2019

Hello Jean,

By now you must have finished your list of all the activities you've dropped and put them in order. I appreciate that we mustn't let our guard down as we get older. I just hope that when I reach your age I'll be as tenacious as you.

As I told you, my parents live on a housing estate. I suppose there might be something comforting about living on an estate where all houses are identical. I was surprised that they wanted to buy a house in the countryside rather than stay in town when they retired. They praised how safe the neighbourhood was, how close the neighbours were, the lovely kitchen, the small garden that required hardly any maintenance, the very practical garage under the house, the "master bedroom with dressing room and walk-in shower". They even bought themselves a home cinema. I don't like housing estates any more than you do, but I understand their choice. They think they got a bargain (they supposedly didn't have to pay any legal fees), and don't care whether their house has character or not. They chose the colour of the shutters (blue or beige), the kitchen (red or white) and the parquet floor (light or dark). What more could they ask for? They hadn't even bargained on this much. They love their home. They find it practical and comfortable.

I'm getting better. When I'm with my baby, I'm not afraid of doing the wrong thing any more. I can talk to her and smile at her without forcing myself or shaking. I tell her how wonderful she is, and how proud I am of her. I tell her how she got her blue eyes from her father, and her black hair from her mother. She'll never know if her maternal grandmother or grandfather have the same, but never mind . . . The sun's finally coming up, Jean! And it's partly thanks to you.

Best wishes,
Juliette

P.S. I forgot to send my last letter to Esther. Would you be so kind as to make a copy and send it to her? Thank you so much.

John is having trouble getting to grips with the last exercise, i.e. projecting himself ten years into the future. To avoid offending Esther, he is making an effort. But he finds the idea ridiculous. He'll write the same letter to both recipients to save time.

In a few days he'll have lunch with his bosses, the two founders of Téléphonie et Digital, to tell them that he's leaving. The weeks after that will be spent with his lawyer, finalizing the details of his departure. Since he made his decision, he can think of nothing else. Resigning is the most profound and exhilarating thing that has happened to him in a long time. His future boils down to this departure. It's overwhelming. He promised himself he wouldn't tell any-one until the negotiations were over. What happens next? It feels like there's a huge black curtain blocking his view. Well, not quite. When the workshop is over, he will have dinner at Camellia. He is delighted to have met Nicolas. There is a ten-year age gap between them, they don't look alike, and they have nothing in common, but in a lot of ways, they are like brothers. Albeit brothers who fall out occasionally. But they respect each other. John wonders if they were just lucky or if it's the same for all the members and whether letter-writing relationships always inspire such confidence and compassion. Did the others enjoy corres-ponding with one another, regardless of whether they had a natural affinity or not? Do letters really have the power to create a special bond between those who write them? What would have happened if he and Nicolas had met at a dinner party? Nicolas would have surely grumbled into his hipster beard: "Who's that arsehole? I hate his sort." And their friendship would never have come about. With Esther, it's different. Unless fate brings them together, there's no reason for them to see each other again. And yet on paper, he likes her. He doesn't know how to arrange it, but he is itching to see her and talk to her. "All things considered, my future is actually looking pretty exciting."

HORIZONS

Jean to Samuel

Verjus-sur-Saône, 30th April 2019

(Here is my letter "ten years later")

Dear Samuel,

I wish you a wonderful 2029. Look how far we've come since our first letters! I had a struggle getting this to you, as post offices are scarce these days. When I think how you used to doubt yourself . . . You've certainly ended up finding your path. You see, Samuel, we never know what life has in store for us. We think we're in control of present and future events, but looking back, we see that the path we end up on is never exactly the one we envisioned, dreamed of or feared. You started moving on with your life the day you stopped grieving for your brother and left guilt behind. Enjoy the ride, but don't take your success for granted; don't assume that things are settled for good. They aren't. If you put your mind to it and if this is what you want, you will experience other great achievements, and other nasty surprises. We only want the former, but they don't come without the latter. This is the price we pay. Don't let your guard down. I have no other advice.

Jean

Samuel to Jean

8th May

Jean,

I saw Mrs Dablon again. I hadn't prepared anything. I don't like thinking about my future because there's nothing I want. It's weird and kind of freaky not being able to imagine yourself anywhere. She didn't seem surprised that I arrived empty-handed. She advised me to do my Baccalaureate via remote learning. She said it's not easy to study on your own, but that students are well monitored and that I've got the ability. It all depends how committed you are.

I'll think about it.

My letter "ten years later":

The other day, I went to see my parents. I don't remember how it came up in the conversation, but we talked about Julian. We all admitted that we are finding it harder and harder to remember his face. It has only taken twelve years for him to become a blur, and for us to forget details such as the sound of his voice. My mum doesn't cry herself to sleep any more, according to my dad. Not that I'm there to hear it anyway.

Here at the sea where I live now, I avoid the news, whether it be the headlines or trivia. I chose this place deliberately as you can pretty much disconnect here. I do my utmost to ensure that nothing can reach me. It's hard though. I can see the Earth dying all around me. The sky is a dirty grey colour that you can't distinguish from the horizon. That same grey that's everywhere, which stops you seeing properly, that makes your eyes sting and your throat burn. Like after a fire, except that the wind doesn't disperse the grey. I call it "cataclysmic grey". The sea is depositing more and more rubbish every day. Some mornings, it gives the impression that it can't make it any more, that it's going to freeze over. It's the sea's way of telling us that it's throwing in the towel and leaving us and our human crap behind. I already know what I'll say just before the sea perishes: "It's eerie, you can't hear the waves any more." We will have lived through the period of lost hope, where there's no way back. Too late, the damage is done, we can't repair it. Do you think any corners of the earth remain unsullied by man?

This is probably the last letter I'll send you. They're making letterboxes obsolete in a few days' time. Just as well I suppose, as it was a nightmare trying to find a stamp. When I asked, I got strange looks. Never mind, we'll see each other soon.

Samuel

Nicolas to Juliette

Paris, 30th April 2019

Juliette, this is my monologue.

My beloved.

She wakes me up at dawn famished and I have to make breakfast. I turn over under the sheets, bury my head in her hair and put my hand on her buttocks. In the winter, when we're dead beat, she curls up on the sofa beside me. We watch a film. I moan about her baggy sweatpants and her big woollen socks. She still looks sexy though. She breaks another plate; she complains about the shoes I left out that she tripped over in the middle of the night. She rightly reminds me that I'm cooking, not writing a doctorate thesis. I rave about her latest breads.

She yanks me by the sleeve to stop me pouncing on the idiot I'm doomed to run into for the rest of my life. She yells at me because, despite my promises, I still haven't started the latest novel she sang the praises of. I sulk because she left early again; I hate waking up without her. In the plane, train or car, on the way to some far-off holiday destination, she kisses me and says: "I'm so happy!" She dances wildly in the middle of the living room, music blaring out. I look at her, I find her hot, smoking hot. When I least expect it, she continues to ask me: "Don't you think we're just so lucky?" She waits for my reply as if our lives depend on it. Like she's asking me this for the first time.

N.

Juliette to Nicolas

Malakoff, 8th May 2019

Nicolas,
My monologue:

I wonder how I came to lose my body. I gazed at myself, naked, in a full-length mirror; not feeling anything. All I could see was a body, which didn't belong to me. As if it was no longer mine. A strange sensation . . . No anger, no vanity. My body has lost its density, its flesh, its buoyancy. I gazed at my breasts, legs, genitals and buttocks with total indifference. I recalled how insecure I used to be about my tummy if I let myself go, my shoulders that I never liked, and my overlapping incisors. None of this bothered me any more. I took care of my body. I knew the routine. I fed it, washed it, clothed it, kept it warm, but it was no longer mine. Since I fell ill, I no longer cared whether men desired me. I no longer thought of my body as a source of seduction and pleasure.

As I got better, my body followed suit, in sync. Its former vibrancy returned, along with its beauty and its imperfections. I studied it, ran my finger over it, caressed it. It became less ethereal and more real.

My libido was no match for the medication and the chemical changes going on inside me. But the good news is that it's back in full force now. I've been awakened, like a sleeping beauty. My stint as a nun and recluse, cowering from the outside world, is over.

I sometimes wonder what I did to restore my body to its former glory.

Juliette

John to Esther and Nicolas

Brussels-Paris, 7th May 2019

Dear Esther and Nicolas,

Ten years later.

I see the sun setting from my window. I no longer think of the pollution and the thick choking air. I forget the silence, the heavy impenetrable solitude, the robots that gatecrashed into our lives, the smart chips that colonized our bodies. I forget that my every word and deed is recorded, analyzed, and stored. I forget how fast this all came about. I forget that I no longer live in fear, that I'm safe. I forget my alerts, and the data on my health, my location and my state of mind. I forget the screens all around. I forget that I sold my soul to the devil and sacrificed my freedom for security. I remember the trees, the endless plains, the deer in the snow, the still lakes, the brightness of the skies, the bats diving into the shed, the rivers I watched from the sky, forging a clean and perfect path across the vast land. I forget that history has been hijacked. I remember our heels walking on the frozen earth, our sticks breaking the ice, the sea unsullied by humans, life's surprises, life's mysteries, idle Sundays in Paris, dead leaves engorged with rainwater, a proud seamstress. And last but not least, us, when it was still possible to save the Earth and ourselves. I vowed not to become an old fool. I am sixty-three years old now. I have no regrets. All this existed and I was lucky enough to have known it.

John

Esther to John

Lille, 11th May 2019
Ten years later.

Dear John,

While tidying away some boxes, I came across our old letters. I don't know if you ever think about the workshop. I do, often. What on earth was I thinking of to come up with such an idea! I may act surprised, but I have fond memories of it.

I read your daughter's latest novel; I liked it. What did you think? It's selling well, on the whole. As you know, readers are few and far between nowadays. Times are tough, but do you remember what I told you at the time? And I do still love my job.

The heat wave is taking its toll here. The fans in the bookshop merely circulate hot air. I'm stifling, and dream of icy rain and snowy mountains. I should have installed air conditioning. There are hardly any fruit and vegetables for sale in the markets, the trees are dying of thirst, water is rationed, the council hasn't planted any flowers in its gardens and parks this year—what's the point, there are no more insects anyway. Permits for driving in town are so hard to obtain now, which means I have trouble getting deliveries. It's one thing after another. But what can you do? Where can you go? The Earth is one big roasting spit!

I saw Nicolas and Juliette two weeks ago; we had dinner together. Nicolas was visiting new vineyards in the region and doing some tastings. I would never have imagined that one day the Lille countryside would be strewn with vineyards! He told me that he had seen you recently, and that you were doing well. I'm a bit peeved that you contacted him and not me. He said you bought new olive trees in Croatia and that your olive oil won another award. I always look out for it in the grocery stores. I shut up shop the first two weeks of August and as usual I forgot to book anywhere for my holidays. Why don't we go away together? There's always Norway, Sweden, Iceland or Greenland?

Esther

Jean to Juliette

Verjus-sur-Saône, 9th May 2019

For Juliette,
monologue.

I think of Hadrian when I make lists.

Buy food for Robert and Alfred.
Why? What would have become of us I wonder? Would we have ended up getting bored with each other? Constantly bickering and at each other's throats? Hating each other? Why do I like making lists?

Sacha books.
As if I could forget, as if I didn't have enough time on my hands.

Baking powder.
I should make a list of everything that would be different if he were still here. It might take the edge off the pain. If he were still here I wouldn't close my eyes and pray to feel his breath on my neck and his arms around me holding me tight one last time. I would look at myself in the mirror more often. I would consider that I'm not aging too badly. I wouldn't listen to loud music, he hated it. I would be calmer.

Buy broom. Order pen paneling.
I wouldn't have repainted one of the living room walls in India Yellow, but in white.
	I would still have a love life (at least I think I would).

Call Darmian refuge Villeurbanne.
My windows wouldn't be in such a bad state. We wouldn't still be living here; he would never have put up with the housing developments.

Carrots/apples/kitchen roll.
I wouldn't talk to myself. I would close the toilet door behind me. I would flush the toilet every time. I wouldn't be so scared of falling seriously ill.

Get ophthalmologist appointment. Phone Diana and the Fontanels for dinner here (24th or 30th?) + garage.
I wouldn't go to Luc's for coffee every morning.

Answer fence quote.
In the evening, I wouldn't try to fall asleep imagining that Hadrian was out and would be back soon. I wouldn't have given up on Aurélie. I'd go on holiday.

Spare set of keys?
I wouldn't have signed up for this workshop. I wouldn't have written a monologue.

Best wishes,
Jean

Juliette to Jean

Malakoff, 14th May 2019

For Jean,
   Monologue on a missed opportunity.

When I woke at dawn, I had only one thing on my mind: going home. Right now! It's urgent! What the hell am I doing here? In this cubbyhole, all alone, without my family. I grab my bag, throw my clothes in a suitcase and go. Unfortunately, things don't work out that way. I need to learn to plan ahead and weigh up the consequences of my actions. What happened afterwards was inevitable.

   Here I am, standing on the pavement with my suitcase in front of our building, frozen to the spot. Is it really wise to barge in while they are still asleep, without warning them first? "Surprise, surprise, it's me!" Why didn't I think of all this before? What will I do once I'm through the door? Will I wake up Nicolas? Will I act as if nothing has happened? Make breakfast? Will I take care of Adele, who'll start crying, asking for her daddy, or Sylvie? All three of them have their own routine which I don't know, or barely know. A bull in a china shop, that's what I'll be. A stranger in my own home. God, I can't handle this . . . I stand there, staring up at our windows, like I'm a stranger, trying to convince myself that I can do it. But no, I can't. I then realize, at this precise moment, that before I can go home, I must write to my parents. I don't know why, or what the connection is, but I must do it in this order. Until I've written to them, I won't have come full circle.

I hadn't noticed that Sylvie had put geraniums on the balconies. They look pretty. I can tell that I am on the edge of tears. I would love to be the person I used to be, capable of making decisions without turning everything into an ordeal. I hate myself. I'm a bag of nerves. I must get out of here. I don't want the concierge or the newsagent to see me with my suitcase, I wouldn't know what to say. If I'd put my brain on standby and not panicked at the last second, I would be home now. It's too late. Taxi!

Juliette

GETAWAY

Samuel to Jean

11th May

Hello Jean,

I know I wrote to you only three days ago, but there's something I am bursting to tell you. My brother kept his travel guide books at the end of the top shelf. There are three of them, and all three are about Japan. I hadn't noticed them until now. Yesterday morning, I flipped through them and realized that Julian had read them from beginning to end. He had circled the names of temples, museums, streets, islands. All the places he would have visited if he had gone there. At least, that's what I'm assuming. It's true that he read a lot of Japanese novels. From looking at these guidebooks, you'd think they belonged to someone who went there every year. Maybe that was his secret. He must have thought that if he got better he would make the trip. At the end, there is a list of Japanese vocabulary. He circled some words too. Maybe he knew what they meant and told no one. In one of the guidebooks, I found an article which Julian had cut out of a newspaper, "Phone conversations with the dead". It's a wicked story, I'll summarize it for you, because it gave me an idea. In the Tohoku region of Japan, the 2011 tsunami killed twenty thousand people, including half of the inhabitants of the village of Otsuchi. A guy called Itaru Sasaki set up a phone booth there, but the phone wires are connected to nothing; that's why it's known as "the wind phone", so messages to the dead can be carried on the wind. He built it in his garden after his cousin died of cancer, to be able to have one-way conversations with him. Then came the tsunami, which swept away his best friend. The day they found his body, two months later, he went into the wind phone booth to talk to him. The other residents started to come to the booth to do the same thing and talk to their own dead. They also started writing to their dead, because he had provided them with a notebook too. This is the eleventh volume apparently. There are photos in these notebooks. Journalists have written articles about this wind phone and foreigners who want to talk or write to their relatives have made the trip there. One journalist writes that, "the wind phone is a kind of substation for the afterlife". They recorded the people in the booth and made a documentary about it. An old man says to his wife: "It's cold today, but I hope you're not cold where you are. Come back soon. Everyone is waiting for you. I will build a house in the same place for us. Eat. Come back to life. Somewhere. Anywhere. I'm so lonely." A father says to his dead son: "It's been five years since the tsunami. If this call reaches you, please listen to us. Sometimes I don't know why I carry on. I want to hear you say 'Dad'." These stories bring tears to my eyes. It seems that in Japan the living talk to the dead, ghosts give signs to the living, and cross over from one dimension to another. The Japanese don't freak out about death, like we do. I like this idea.

When I finished reading the article, I looked at the date. A shiver ran down my spine. It was only three weeks before Julian died. I laid awake thinking about it the whole night, and then I made a decision. That evening, my parents were waiting for me for dinner, and I handed them the pages. My voice was quivery, I was nervous, and very uncomfortable. I felt stupid, but I had to go through with it: "This is an article I found in his room in one of his guidebooks on Japan. Look when it was written. I wish the three of us could go there. I think that's what he wanted."

I couldn't bring myself to utter my brother's name. It's idiotic. That's the kind of blockage I get with my parents and it does my head in. This trip would be good for that, letting the three of us get together and talk. Talk about Julian and remember the good times without destroying ourselves. And move on, too. My dad took the article. My mum stood up to get closer. They read it together, her standing, leaning over him. My dad finished before her. He said nothing, got up and went to lock himself in the bathroom, without so much as glancing at me. My mum was crying, wiping her eyes all the time. The tears made it hard for her to read. I knew that if they said no, it wouldn't be about money. They wouldn't understand, they wouldn't want to chase some deluded fantasy of mine (precisely what it is) or such a morbid prospect scares them. My parents aren't wealthy, they live modestly, and our holidays never cost much. We always went to my maternal grandparents in the Dordogne, that was all. We didn't dare travel abroad, because of Julian. My dad came out of the bathroom. He had been crying too. He looked at me: "If your mother agrees, we can go this summer . . . Margaux?" She looked at me and smiled. "A trip to Japan with my men, I'd like nothing better. Where exactly is this wind phone? Can you show us the guidebooks?"

I wondered if there were two or three men in my mother's life. Logically, the answer is three.

Samuel

Jean to Samuel

Verjus-sur-Saône, 16th May 2019

Dear Samuel,
I saw on the internet what the wind phone looks like. It's pretty with its green roof and white walls. I can imagine you

inside . . . Bravo! You demonstrated tremendous courage
in suggesting this trip to your parents. You'll go there with
them and then start your Baccalaureate. It's a super plan, and
you're more than capable of it.

Logically speaking, this is the last letter I shall be sending
you as part of our workshop. If you would like us to continue
corresponding, I would be more than happy to. Do tell me
about your trip to Japan if nothing else. Especially the wind
phone. I look forward to hearing from you. The world is your
oyster, Samuel. You've grasped that you have to be brave and
audacious in life to get what you want.

Stand tall and walk in the light.

Jean

In the weeks that followed, she waited in vain for Samuel's
reply. As soon as the workshop ended, it appeared that the
young man had put down his pen, folded away his paper
napkins and forgotten all about Jean. She is disappointed.
She wonders if he hasn't written to her for three months because he was prevented from doing so. No, it's impossible,
she says to herself. He didn't have to tell her about his latest
initiative. She would have liked to carry on writing to him, at
least to say goodbye. "This is the last letter I will send you,"
he wrote in his "ten years later" letter. And indeed it was.

Jean to Juliette

Verjus-sur-Saône, 17th May 2019

Hello Juliette,

Esther wants us to teleport ourselves into 2029. I refuse
to. I am sixty-seven years old and can think of far more up-
lifting scenarios than imagining my life when I'm almost

eighty. Time flies, I have no desire to speed it up. At best I'll be diminished, at worst I'll be ill or dead. Sounds like a bundle of laughs! If we delve too far into the past or project ourselves into the future, we risk going belly up. Let's enjoy the present. Keeping track of the daily activities I have abandoned over the years and trying to reinstate them is enough for me.

I'm glad your parents are happy in their house. I wouldn't dream of begrudging them that. It's the property developers and other professionals in the chain that I blame. If they at least tried to build houses with character and a nice view, your parents would be even happier. To look at trees instead of bins, to hear birdsong instead of traffic, and to live in a house that you find aesthetically pleasing, and which isn't a carbon copy of your neighbour's, is fundamental to our well-being.

This week was the last week of our workshop. I hope you will still send me your letter "ten years later".

I wanted to thank you for trusting me. I hope we'll have the opportunity to meet again. I would be delighted to have you over to stay. I'm sure Adele would be fine here. You're very welcome, all three of you, or just the two of you, which-ever you prefer. I have plenty of room for you all. I won't bother you any further.

Jean

Juliette to Jean

Malakoff, 21st May 2019
Ten years later.

Dear Jean,

Since my depression eleven years ago, I am totally an-chored in the present. To have lived through such horror makes me appreciate every second of happiness that comes my way. And the nostalgia you get when it's over is even more intense now.

"Mum, what are you thinking about?" asks Adele when she sees me daydreaming. "Nothing in particular, my angel, I'm a little tired." That's not true, I'm thinking about my old demons, when I diced with death and felt it lurking all around me. But I survived. Since then, my life has taken on other colours and another dimension. It has more depth and is on a more solid footing than before. I'm alive, but I know what it feels like to have a brush with death, or rather the terror it triggers in you and the way it sneers in your face. Plus that metallic taste in your mouth, the body you can't control, the legs that give way, the trembling hands, the cotton wool mind. I can't forget. No one is ever prepared for such a dreadful experience. And no one comes out of it unscathed.

This morning, from our balcony, Nicolas and I watched Adele go off to school. It's her first day back. She stopped on the pavement, looked up at us, smiled and blew us a kiss, before turning and disappearing around the corner. I closed the window. We looked at each other. He took me in his arms. I kissed him and told him I loved him. We were thinking the same things and didn't need to say a word: Adele, our only daughter, my parents, his parents, what we have been through. And also the coffee that was brewing in the kitchen. And don't ask me why, but I was thinking of the Berlin Wall.

Best regards,
Juliette

P.S. Stop thinking you're bothering me. If you were, I would have stopped writing to you. Thanks for the invite. What about you, when are you coming to Paris?

22nd May

Dear Mum and Dad,

I'm sorry. I know you well enough to know how worried you are. I wouldn't wish what happened to me (post-partum depression) on anyone. I'm supposed to tell you that I'm better, that I didn't go through all this for nothing, and that I've come out of it stronger. But I'm not going to say that. Because I prefer the person I was before. To become who I am today, I had to endure too much suffering.

There's no way I could have seen you in the midst of all the turmoil. It would have been too painful. You have done nothing wrong, but seeing you would have been a reminder of my own birth story. And I couldn't have handled it, so I had to keep you away from me. I couldn't have added chaos to chaos. I'm sorry, as absolutely none of this is your fault. You have nothing to blame yourselves for, absolutely nothing.

My pregnancy and the arrival of Adele were really difficult for me. Having a baby forced me to confront my own trauma surrounding being abandoned at birth, which I hadn't pre-viously acknowledged. It took up all my headspace. For the first time in my life I fell apart because of this woman (hard for me to consider her as my "mother"!) who didn't leave me a thing, not a single word, object, or farewell letter when she abandoned me. Adele was an echo back to this past. I was unable to look after her, love her, protect her. I couldn't sleep, I couldn't eat. Deep down I loved my baby, but at the same time, I began to hate her.

Nothing will ever be the same again.

Thanks to you both, I had the most wonderful childhood. The best childhood ever. I was lucky. Very lucky.

Knowing that you were waiting for me to come home to see Adele again, because, as you so beautifully put it to

Nicolas, "it's our way of telling Juliette that we love her and we're waiting for her", was of immense help in my recovery process. I can't imagine what you must have been going though.

I can't wait to hug and kiss you both.
With all my love,
Juliette

Silence prevails in the flat. Juliette lifts her suitcase to avoid rolling it on the floor. The bedroom door is slightly open. Nicolas is sleeping. The light barely filters through the shutters. It is a very dark and moonless night. Nicolas turns his back to her. He is sleeping deeply; she can tell from his heavy, regular breathing. She stands beside the bed. She slowly takes off her clothes, one by one, her body trembling, without taking her eyes off Nicolas. She lies down beside him, presses her breasts against his back, wraps her legs around his, strokes his face, his hair, his chest, his stomach, his manhood. Nicolas grabs her hand, kisses it, breathes on it in the hollow of his palm. He turns around; he feels her breath on his face, he recognizes her scent, the rosemary in her hair, the rose and sandalwood on her skin. In the darkness he can detect her wide-open eyes, her big smile, and can feel her heart beating wildly. He has waited so long for this moment.

nico-esthover@free.fr, juju-esthover@free.fr,
jean.dupuis5@laposte.net, john.beaumont2@orange. com,
samsam-cahen@free.fr

Subject: The end of our workshop

Dear all,

This email marks the end of our workshop. I hope it met your expectations and that you noticed how you progressed over the weeks. I was dying to read your letters. In all honesty, I hadn't expected to be so moved by them. You all played the game, each and every one of you, and put in tremendous effort. One question came up several times, on the phone or by email: "Were we just lucky in finding the right pen pals or would we have had a different but equally intense letter writing relationship with others?" Given that writing to each other as part of a workshop automatically encourages you to get along with your correspondent, I don't know the answer to that. I would only say, now that I know you a little, that luck did play a part. But it wasn't just luck. Again, with no exceptions, you were thoughtful and attentive, and trusted and believed in each other. This is no mean feat. It played a huge role in the success of our workshop. You are from all walks of life, so disagreements, frictions, and frustrations were inevitable, but you dealt with them intelligently. We were open and honest with each other, and this in my opinion was our trump card.

I wish to thank you for believing in my crazy project. I sincerely hope that it has made you want to continue to put pen to paper and write to your nearest and dearest. Even if they do live just a stone's throw away.

Esther

I went to pick up Raphael at the train station. I couldn't wait for him to arrive. Not that I had anything to look forward to. He was coming to help me sort out my father's things. I refused to turn his flat into a shrine. It was time for me to move on. "I have to clear it out and put it up for sale. I can't do it on my own." Raphael accepted without the slightest hesitation. Pia had kindly offered to help us but I refused. I didn't know how I would handle it or cope.

I had reserved a table at Bloempot. We went straight there, after the station. Raphael thought I was on edge. I told him that my writing workshop had just ended and that I hadn't heard from John. I was annoyed at myself for having been so hard on him in my letters. He had written to me that he was lonely and was thinking of "evaporating". We joked about it, but the more time went by, the more seriously I took his outburst. Raphael found this story of evaporating totally ridiculous. He laughed. "What kind of crap is that?" I got on my high horse. I told him about this phenomenon, which is common in Japan, backed up by figures which I've since forgotten. "I am afraid for him," I confessed. He went silent and then said: "You like this man, I can tell. This is good, even if he has messed with your head. What I can also see is that since your father's death, you are terrified of losing the people you love. Like they're suddenly going to just disappear. You must stop this." I told him that he was exaggerating, that he was wrong. He smiled at me.

The next day we got up early, and had a king size breakfast as always: coffee, freshly squeezed orange juice, toast, butter, jam, honey, squares of dark chocolate, scrambled eggs, muesli. We left the house with full stomachs. I had anticipated a lot of boxes and bin bags. I had only been back to my father's home once since he died, to fetch my letters. It was a beautiful flat, with large, bright rooms and beautiful eighteenth-century furniture. He had good taste. The parquet floor creaked under our steps. I was right not to let my daughter come. Almost every object reminded me of something and set me off crying. Despite my grief, I was extremely efficient. I gritted my teeth and sorted through his stuff mercilessly. I made a pile of things I was throwing out, and another pile of things I was giving to charity. A removal man would come by within the week to take my mother's statues to a friend who would store them in Dunkirk, in a barn adjoining his house. Most of the pieces were monumental. My mother sculpted women's bodies with voluptuous breasts, broad thighs, and plump buttocks. Her men were Hercules with bulging muscles, strong chests and, there's no other word for it, *bulging sex organs*. Statues of classical construction and others of a formidable contemporaneity. Her large, beautiful and disturbing cats were reminiscent of the felines of the Japanese artist Miyazaki. I was planning to bring two of them back to my flat. I gave one to Raphael, his favourite. I wondered how my mother's art would have evolved if she had lived. I insisted that Raphael take anything he wanted. It's strange, but he only took the pack of cigarettes that was still lying on my father's desk: his Marlboro Reds. And a picture in his bookcase of his mother and my father sitting in a boat. They are looking at the lens and laughing. He must be ten years old, and she is eight. I gave him the photo albums, adding that I would collect them later, when I had the strength to look at them.

In the evening, we had dinner at my place, then went out for a beer. I told him about Samuel and how in one of his letters, he wrote that clearing out his dead brother's room had been more painful than the burial itself. Within the space of a few hours, his whole life had disappeared, it had been boxed and taped up. I understand now what he felt. That flash of insight that nobody remembers. Oh, the insignificance of our lives . . . And man's vanity in believing his life is important.

REUNION

The last letter John wrote to Esther was dated 7ᵗʰ May, just over a month ago. Since then, he and his lawyer have been negotiating the terms of his departure from Téléphonie et Digital. He didn't call to thank her. Nor did he call back after the message she left him. He likes the sound of her voice. He listened to her message several times. He had no idea she was worried. He thought she was calling to say goodbye.

John wants to see Esther, nothing else matters. If he can't, he'll lock himself away in his flat, take sleeping pills to blot it out, and let fate run its course. He booked three nights at the Clarance Hotel in Lille. That's exactly what he needs this morning, to get on a train and leave Paris. Before meeting Esther, he wants to observe her from afar. If he goes to the bookshop he runs the risk of her recognizing him. She has his picture. *Stupid old geezer, at fifty-three, it's pathetic. Have you nothing better to do than play hide and seek with her?* he reproaches himself, once safely in the train. He's cheating really, but his little game delights and excites him.

After dropping his suitcase at the hotel, he visits the city. He will try his luck with Esther tomorrow. He dines alone in a noisy and friendly café. He is less enthusiastic than she was about the local speciality: chips with smelly cheese. He is delighted to have all the time in the world to stroll aimlessly around at his leisure.

He had a restless night. The sun woke him up early, so he decided to go for a run, a new resolution. He puts on a pair of shorts, his brand-new Nike running shoes and goes for a run in the Citadelle park. His performance is abysmal, much worse than he expected. He has an excuse: the overwhelming heat. He buys a newspaper on the way back to his hotel, showers and has breakfast in his room. He enters the address of the bookshop on his mobile and leaves the hotel. He's impatient to see Esther, even if only through her bookshop windows. And find out what this strange girl looks like. This strange girl whom he confided in for three whole months, at night, from his plane.

The front of the bookshop is duck blue and the sign "A must read" is spelled out in mustard yellow letters. He doesn't linger. If he stands there on the opposite pavement, he'll be spotted. The glare of the sun prevents him from seeing inside. He'll wait for Esther on Dutilleul Square, where she usually has lunch. If he's lucky, she'll be there. He, who had to reread his diary several times to remember his appointments, can remember everything she told him about herself, every little detail. He has no illusions. The Esther of his imagination has a face, a body, a look, a complexion, and clothes that are probably far removed from reality. But he'll recognize her. She'll sit on a bench; open a book and he'll know.

In the meantime, he strolls around the neighbourhood and in the public gardens. He discovers the green alder of the subalpine regions and the red oak of America and is surprised to see succulent plants in a northern European city. John chooses a bench, a little out of the way, where he can observe all the comings and goings. Around 12:15 pm, it gets busier. Couples, groups of happy talkative girls, mothers with children, two studious boys, businessmen eating their sandwiches in a hurry, eyes riveted to their phones, but no single woman with a book. Well, there's one, but she's too young to be Esther. John gives up hope. He ponders whether to return to the bookshop, when suddenly she crosses the street, and heads towards the square. It's impossible not to notice her. She is tall and slim, her pretty face is covered in freckles. Her long red hair falls on to her red jacket. She is wearing jeans and high black leather boots, which look incongruous in this heat. She walks briskly in John's direction but forks at the last moment and sits down on a bench just behind his.

This sort of woman breaks the hearts of men like me he thinks, without daring to turn around. She is nothing like he imagined, but he's sure it's her. Everything comes back to him now. Her mother's red hair, her liking for red jackets, her refusal to listen to the weather forecast to know what to wear. *I shall count to a hundred and twenty and turn around* he decides. *If the woman with the red hair and the out of place leather boots is reading, then it's her.* If so, he'll approach her.

Jean receives a parcel from Juliette, containing a little note:

"Hello Jean, here is a sneak preview of my latest gourmet surprise. I hope it didn't get damaged in transit. It's my 'Jean brioche' flaked with candied white raisins, roasted walnuts and cappuccino, with a lightly caramelized coating. I'm back home now. Juliette." Every morning, Nicolas takes a look at the bookings. He spots the name John Beaumont. A table for two, tonight, Friday 20th September. At the beginning of May, the two men had stopped writing to each other, without saying goodbye. Juliette came home and Nicolas forgot about John. For his part, John negotiated his departure, took a train to Lille and forgot about Nicolas. While he was on holiday in Noirmoutier that summer, Nicolas promised himself that he would contact John and invite him to Camellia. It's well into the new school year and Nicolas still hasn't got round to doing it. Too late now, John took the lead. The restaurant owner normally greets his customers at the end of the evening, but he makes an exception for John. At precisely

8:30 pm, Nicolas is informed of his arrival. John's punctuality doesn't surprise him. He joins him at reception. He imagined John to be taller. They smile at each other from afar, a little embarrassed and emotional. Both are thinking the same thing, namely that it's easy to confide in a stranger in writing, but much harder in real life.

Nicolas shook John's hand and patted him heartily on the back: "I'm so happy to see you!" In the photos, he hadn't noticed how blue John's eyes were. The woman accompanying him turned around to face him. Oh my God, it's Esther!

Esther and John chose the tasting menu. They weren't able to try his springtime *je ne sais quoi* with green asparagus, sea urchins, taramasalata and lemongrass, as it's out of season.

The next day at breakfast, Nicolas was giggling to himself.

"What's so funny?" asks Juliette.

"You remember I told you that John dined at Camellia yesterday? Guess who he brought with him?"

"No idea."

"Esther!"

"Esther, from the workshop? Are they dating?"

"Yep. It's been three months now. He went to see her in Lille, and BING!"

"That's good, isn't it?"

"Good? It's bloody awesome, you mean! If you'd seen my face when I realized, you'd have been in fits like they were. In fact, I haven't actually seen John Beaumont depressed. Oh and they've invited us to Lille. What do you say?"

"Yes, I'd like that . . . Was that Adele? I'll go and see if she's awake. Has he moved to Lille?"

"No. They split their time between Lille and Paris. He's the one who travels—he quit his job."

"She's still sleeping. Were you able to talk?"

"Yes. They waited for me after closing."

"Was it nice to see them?"

"Very. There were a few awkward moments, but they didn't last. I didn't know John before, but it's as if quitting work and falling in love have totally transformed him. Don't forget, one letter from this guy could plunge you straight into the abyss. As Esther says, "It's proof that John has a certain talent.""

"Did you talk about the workshop again?"

"Yes, we did. I told her that Jean spent a weekend with us in Paris and that we had invited her to the restaurant. She was delighted for her. She thinks that Jean is very lonely, the contrary of what she wants us to believe. And she reminded me that we hadn't written our "ten years later" letters. She can't comprehend that it's weird for us to keep writing to each other now that you're back."

"Is she going to do another workshop?"

"Ah, I didn't ask. But she did mention that she'd like to put all our letters together and pitch them to a publisher—with our consent of course. In her own words we are "one hell of a motley crew". She said the literary exercise turned into a life lesson from which we all emerged transformed."

"Would you agree to it?"

"Why not. What about you?"

"Hmm, I'm not sure."

THE WIND PHONE

15th September

Hello Jean,

I'm back from Japan. We flew out on 18th August, as the flights were a bit cheaper in the second half of the month. When my parents saw the price of the trip, even with two stopovers, I thought they were going to back out. But they didn't. It was literally awesome! We arrived in Tokyo, where we stayed for four days. One of my dad's former colleagues put us up. He lived quite a way from the must-see places so we had to hop on a few buses to visit them, but it was worth it. Tokyo was my favourite city. My parents preferred Kyoto. I loved the revolving counter sushi bars, so did my mum. We went right to the top of the towers, visited the electric district, department stores, kawaii stores, game centres, parks, temples and a cemetery. It was my mum who insisted on going to the cemetery. Just a week before we flew out, she didn't know anything about Japanese death culture, but after googling it, she came across several blogs that discussed it. She became obsessed with it, although she didn't tell us at the time. She told me afterwards, in a cemetery in Kyoto, that she liked the idea of the living talking to the dead, and of the little statues dressed in red to whom offerings are made, which you see everywhere in the cemeteries there. Each one watches over a dead person. There are altars, lanterns, towers with bells, wooden plates where you can write your prayers. It sounds goofy but I actually found it all made me feel very much *alive*. In their cemeteries, you don't just wallow in misery and unhappiness. Of course, you are sad, but you're also at peace. It makes you want to believe in spirits and signs. My mum and I see eye to eye on this one. We like the idea of the dead keeping one foot in the world of the living. In France, we like to mourn our dead, remember them, clean their graves and put flowers on them, but the idea of them disturbing us gives us the creeps. My dad came with us, but it wasn't really his thing. After that, we went to Kyoto by train, the famous bullet train which they call Shinkansen. We rented a flat through my father's friend. It wasn't big, but it had such a cool layout. We've decided to get the same in Villejuif. And we're going to decorate it in a Japanese style. My dad loved visiting the temples. I got bored of them really quickly. They are impressive but when you've seen one, you've seen them all. As each day passed, the tension with my parents eased, despite us not mentioning Julian. We were afraid it would set one of us off crying and spoil the trip. The way we communicated made us appear like strangers who were getting to know each other. One morning, I announced that I wanted to do my Baccalaureate via remote learning. They hadn't asked me how it went with Mrs Dablon. I even wondered whether my dad had forgotten. I suppose I only announced it to impress them and make them proud of me. How lame, yes I know, but once I said it, I had to go through with it. Besides, the idea kind of enamoured me. I don't think I could have done them any greater favour. My dad said he had colleagues who could help me.

Then we had to go to Otsuchi. That was the whole point of the trip, but I think we all found the idea a bit silly in the end. We didn't dare say this to each other, so we took a train there. When we arrived, we looked around a bit, but all we could think about was Julian and the wind phone. We asked how to get there. It was very hot, but windy. I showed the pictures of the newspaper article and people immediately pointed me in the direction of a hilltop, a little further on. I led the way, walking in front of my parents. Suddenly, there it was, looming in front of me. The famous wind phone, a white telephone booth with a green roof, standing in the middle of a garden. I saw a black, disconnected rotary dial telephone on a metal shelf with a notebook beside it. My mum came up behind me, looked at the booth and laughed nervously. She looked up at the sky. It was cloudy. My dad walked around the booth, then said, "It's rather incredible, this phone in the middle of nowhere. I don't know what you want to do right now, Sam. It's going to take me a little while before I can do it. I'm going to sit down in a corner, right over there, and draw it." We watched him walk away. We were happy that the phone booth inspired him to sketch it. I asked my mum if she wanted to go first. I knew we wouldn't go in together; we weren't ready for that. Impossible, we were too embarrassed, too coy; besides too much distance had come between us over the years to talk to a dead person together, and cry together. She replied: "No, you go ahead if you want. But if you prefer to wait, no problem, we've got the whole day. I don't want to spoil the moment." I didn't dare ask her what she meant by that, which would determine whether her experience in the wind phone booth was positive or not. I was ready, in my own way, to say whatever came into my head, without calculating my words beforehand. I entered the booth and closed the door behind me. I guessed that my parents were watching me. I turned my back to them and closed my eyes. It smelled of wood, grass, damp. I picked up the phone and put it to my ear. Of course, Julian wasn't going to start talking to me. I thought about the people they had interviewed for the newspaper article. One said, "Let me hear you say 'Dad'." Another, "I want to hear your reply, but I can't hear anything." We all hoped, but all knew we would get nothing back. Still, I must admit there was an eerie atmosphere inside. Maybe because of all the people who had stood in that small booth that welcomed hope and pain, life and afterlife, and words spoken to our dead ones. I swear there was. Everyone could feel it.

Maybe if my parents hadn't been so close by, I would have broken down and cried. As things stood, I wouldn't let myself. But I did talk to Julian. My head was all over the place.

"Hey, Ju, look, we made it! Coming all the way here, we took you with us. I hope I understood right and that this is what you wanted. I read your books and put them back exactly as I found them when I finished. You gave me a hard time, you know, but I get it now. I probably would have been the same if I'd gone down with cancer. We did have some good times together though, remember? I have some great memories of us at Grandma and Grandpa's. Our tree house, playing hide and seek, and football with Dad. And the pool when they opened the water slide and the stories Mum read to us. Please give me a sign and let me know that you're okay wherever you are. Or better still, let Mum and Dad know. I've made a decision: I'm not going to feel guilty about your death any more. I've got no reason to. I'm sure you agree with that. Now I'm going to write a message in the notebook. It's for you and Mum and Dad too." I wrote, "We've got to learn to live without you. Three instead of four. I'll miss you forever." I left the booth. And that was it.

My dad was sketching. My mum joined me. I told her I wrote a message in the phone book and that she could read it. She asked me if it made me feel better. I said yes. She smiled at me. She went into the booth as well. She picked up the receiver. I sat down on the bench and gazed at the landscape. I felt calm. I would have loved to see the owner of the cabin, but he didn't come. My mum stayed inside for at least twenty minutes. When she came out, she walked over and sat down next to me. We didn't look at each other. She took my hand, pressed it against her cheek and thanked me. I turned around. My dad was in the booth, pasting his drawing in the notebook. He had brought some Sellotape with him. He had it all planned. I don't think he tried to talk to Julian. He came out right away, said I could go look at the drawing if I wanted to. I went back in. He had drawn the booth and the trees around it. I was inside the booth but not alone. Julian was standing behind me and hugging me. We were dressed the same, with the clothes I was wearing that day, and we were smiling. The difference between us was that my father had accentuated the outline of my body while Julian's was rather blurred. There is a photo of us two as little ones, posing in the same position. I had forgotten about it. I wonder what became of it. My mum didn't write anything in the notebook. I took a photo of the drawing with my phone.

Before we flew to Japan, I nearly packed one of Julian's novels by a Japanese author. It seemed logical, but I respected what I had told myself, to read them one after the other starting from left to right. So I began with *The World According to Garp* by John Irving. On the plane home, I read the accident scene when Garp is in the car with his two sons, Walt and Duncan. Walt dies. Duncan loses his brother. I took that as a sign.

I hope you're well.
Samuel

ACKNOWLEDGEMENTS

I would particularly like to thank Éric and Lou. And my thanks also go to my godmother, Anne-Marie, and Geneviève Metge and Florentine Rey, both authors themselves who run writers' workshops in Lyon with the Paragraphe literary association, as well as Natalie Gonzalez, for her support. And last but not least, thank you to my dear editor, Caroline Lépée.

"I'm the eggshell that was smashed to pieces to release the chick." One mother's experience of post-partum depression as described in the book *Tremblements de mères: Le visage caché de la maternité* (L'Instant présent).

The article "Phone conversations with the dead" appeared in the French newspaper *L'Obs* (14th June 2019).

The question "What battles are you fighting?" is taken from *Garçon, de quoi écrire* by John d'Ormesson and François Sureau (Gallimard/Folio).